SMOKE AND MIRRORS BOOK 2

MYSTERY AT THE BAY SANDS HOTEL

JAN JONES

To Sylvia,

Happy Reading!

Jan Jones

SMOKE AND MIRRORS BOOK 2

MYSTERY AT THE BAY SANDS HOTEL

JAN JONES

When the rich play, they play for keeps

~The second in the Smoke and Mirrors mystery series~

,

DEDICATION

Mystery at the Bay Sands Hotel is dedicated to the resilience of the human spirit, at home and abroad

DRAMATIS PERSONAE

Staff

Lucy Brown ~ a chambermaid with a split personality

Irene Trent ~ a chambermaid with an abrasive personality

Fauntleroy Delaney ~ manager of the Bay Sands Hotel

Myrtle Smith ~ Mr Delaney's niece, bookkeeper, general factotum

Mrs Ryland ~ Head housekeeper

Grigory ~ senior waiter

Pyotr ~ an overqualified gardener

a surprising number of indoor and outdoor staff

Hotel Guests

Jack Sinclair ~ devil-may-care playboy

Charles Bridgewater ~ Jack's oldest friend

Edward Carter ~ very rich industrialist

Veronique Carter ~ his daughter

Phoebe Sugar ~ society reporter

Thalia Portman ~ man-eater

Mr & Mrs Lester ~ city financier and his society wife

Julie and Amanda Lester ~ flapper twins approaching their weddings

Theo Nicholson and Hubert Jarmaine ~ their amiable bridegrooms

Rupert Manners, Earl of Elvedon ~ theatrical dilettante

Mr & Mrs Mackenzie ~ construction magnate and wife

Mr Forrest ~ a banker

Gustav Karlsson ~ owner of merchant ships

Xavier Hilliard ~ upmarket moneylender

Gina Bianca ~ film actress

Ronnie Oaks ~ Miss Bianca's manager

Jimmy Ward ~ Miss Bianca's admirer

Tufty Thomas ~ foolish nonentity

sundry socialites bent on amusement

The Police

Detective Chief Inspector Curtis ~ of Scotland Yard

Detective Inspector Maynard ~ of Scotland Yard

Detective Sergeant Fenn ~ photography expert

Detective Sergeant Draper ~ fingerprint expert

Sergeant Pine ~ local police

Constable Williams ~ local police

CHAPTER ONE

Bay Sands Hotel, Lincolnshire coast, England, 1927

Lucy Brown finished making her penultimate bed of the morning and wondered if anyone would notice if she lay down on it for a short nap.

The answer, she thought glumly, was that Mrs Ryland would. She could just imagine how the conversation with the head housekeeper would go.

"Perhaps you can explain, Miss Brown, why you found it necessary to disarrange your handiwork in room 17?"

"I was checking the mattress was up to standard, Mrs Ryland."

"Very commendable. Collect your wages at the office on your way out. I wish I could say it has been a pleasure to have you with us for such a short time."

Lucy sighed and hoisted her basket of cleaning equipment. She took a last look around the room. Twin beds with crisp cotton sheets turned down a regulation seven inches at the top, two blankets on each (summer on the east coast of England not being so very reliable as far as temperature was concerned) topped with eiderdowns and boldly patterned bedspreads in blue, grey and silver curves. Everything as it should be, and all in accordance with the Bay Sands Hotel chambermaid handbook.

This was one of the luxe rooms with wide windows and a bay view. A glass door opened on to a balcony, discreetly railed off from the balconies to left and right, thus creating an unbroken line when viewed from outside. Inside, the curtains matched the bedspreads, and the carpet picked up the blue and grey theme. Lucy privately considered waking up in here would be akin to clinging to a life raft in the middle of the ocean, but she wasn't an expert in hotel decor.

Dubious design aside, it was a comfortably appointed room. There was a capacious wardrobe, a modern dressing table with a large round mirror, and a table in the same ash-veneered plywood over by the window where upholstered chairs in blue and grey invited guests to take their ease. The private bathroom was a masterpiece of white enamel and gleaming chrome. Lucy herself had been responsible for the gleam.

It was a far cry from her room in the staff block which was exactly twice the width of the bed and shared a window with the room next door. Her fellow chambermaid Irene had pointed out they were hardly in their quarters long enough for the size of them to be a problem. Who needed space when you were asleep?

Now Lucy headed out into the corridor to see Irene emerging from the room opposite with her arms full of bedding.

"Faugh," said Irene, dumping it in the wicker laundry hamper. "You wouldn't think people who are rich enough to book here could be such pigs."

"Careful," cautioned Lucy. "Mrs R will hear you."

"I don't care," said Irene, but she lowered her voice. "I had to open the windows while I cleaned and the wind is perishing. I can't think why I stay in this rotten job."

Because you tried the bright lights once and got burnt. Because you have a child and an invalid mother to support, you are twenty-eight years old and there aren't enough lucrative careers in the faded bywater of Kingsthorpe that you can afford to be choosy.

"Because you can't bear the thought of me having to clean all two dozen of our rooms by myself," she said aloud. "Selfless, that's what you are, Irene, selfless."

The other girl gave a reluctant grin. "That's me finished anyway. I hope Mrs R passes us. It's my half-day and I want to catch the bus into town. Gives me a bit longer with May than if I walk. You coming in?"

Lucy shook her head. "I'm off to the dunes. I've got letters to write. I might as well do them somewhere nice."

"Suit yourself. I can't say I see the attraction."

"That's because you grew up here. To a city girl like me, it's rather beautiful."

"And as soon as your folks write to say 'come home, all is forgiven', you'll be off."

"But with lovely memories," pointed out Lucy.

"You're easily pleased, that's all I can say. I wonder who we'll get in our rooms this week. They ought to be good tippers, oughtn't they, if they're here for the grand opening ball? Only the best clientele, that's what Mr Delaney said."

Lucy shrugged. "We'll find out." She drew Irene out of sight as a corpulent businessman emerged from a room further down the corridor with a lady who was almost certainly not his wife. "Good. That's my last room. I do wish people would leave on time. I must have worn out a track on this carpet going back and forth waiting for the guests to vacate them."

"It was worse at the Savoy," said Irene. "We weren't allowed to be seen by the guests at all. We had to use poky back corridors and keep our eyes glued to the cracks in the doors."

"Who did they think cleaned the rooms? The fairies?"

"Probably." The couple passed by, the man looking satisfied, the woman looking bravely sophisticated. Irene made a face. "More fool her. I hope she's putting something away against the day he says thanks for the dance, but he can't leave his wife and kiddies. Here's Mrs R. I'll be late back so you'll have to tell me what our new guests are like over breakfast tomorrow."

Lucy moved briskly to her last room. As it happened, she already knew who would be on their floor this week because she had taken the trouble to make friends with the girl in the office. Lucy's mother, who had fought a losing battle to turn her daughter into a biddable copy of herself, was fond of saying a smile wins more than a frown. Lucy, whilst disagreeing with all her mother's plans for her (stay at home, marry a nice young man, start a family) had nevertheless found this to be not only true, but extremely useful.

Irene, in contrast, never took the trouble to be friendly to anyone. Then again, she didn't have an ulterior motive behind her choice of occupation.

Stylishly painted in maroon with blue detailing, and with a uniformed chauffeur to match, the Bay Sands Hotel charabanc waiting at Kingsthorpe railway station contributed to the guests' comfort from the moment of arrival. Mentally congratulating the management on their foresight, Jack Sinclair gazed with interest over the open side of the vehicle as they completed the short journey and pulled to a stop outside the blinding white frontage of the hotel.

He lost no time in jumping down to open the front passenger door. The driver looked askance at this usurpation of his own duties and hurried to descend to the road to open the other doors himself.

In the front seat, the young woman who had been the last to embark handed Jack her capacious holdall and stepped elegantly out.

"Ever the gentleman, Sinclair," guffawed Tufty Thomas from the rearmost bench seat. "Going to help with my luggage too?"

"Only if you've taken to wearing skirts," quipped the wag next to him, and was overcome by his own wit.

Jack ignored them and smiled at the young woman. She was a slender bobbed blonde in her late twenties wearing a pink cloche and a loose white coat worn open over a low-belted pink day dress. "May I carry your bag?" he asked politely.

"Sweet of you," she murmured, retrieving it from him, "but I prefer to handle it myself. I'm a society reporter. One slip of my photographic equipment and my commission goes down by half."

"Jack Sinclair. Pleased to meet you," he said, extending his hand.

"Phoebe Sugar." She rested her white-gloved hand in his. A frisson of warmth ran up his arm from his palm to his biceps.

"Nice," she said ambiguously, then walked towards the hotel. Jack watched her, admiring her smooth stride.

"*By* your leave, sir," said the driver pointedly, moving past him to help down the languorous, heavy-lidded lady who had been sitting next to Miss Sugar.

Jack stepped hastily out of the way. He knew Thalia Portman of old. Not for the world would he encroach on the chauffeur's preserves here.

"Mine are the red Moroccan suitcases," said Mrs Portman in a husky murmur, keeping hold of the driver's arm. "You are new since my last visit, aren't you? Tell me, do you do private tours of the coast at all? It's so marvellously rugged and wild."

"I'm afraid I am employed by the management, madam," said the driver, signalling to a hotel porter and contriving to sound regretful. "Town and back, and group sightseeing only. The reception desk will be able to arrange a private car if you wish for one. The garage by the golf course hires out comfortable chauffeured touring vehicles."

"Shame," she said, letting her hand trail slowly down his arm.

"Enjoy your stay, madam. Thank you, madam." The driver closed his hand on her tip and hurried to lift her suitcases down from the dickey at the back.

"I see the merry widow is starting as she means to go on," observed Tufty, arriving by Jack's side and holding on to his hat in the breeze.

"It certainly looks like it," said Jack.

"Lord, it's bracing on the coast. I always forget. Nice beach though. Have to get into the swimming togs tomorrow."

"Rather," said Jack. "It's a pity the tide is too far out today. I'll see you in the lounge later, I expect."

"Or the bar," said Tufty. "That looks like a jolly cocktail terrace over at the side."

"Very smart," agreed Jack. "There is a casino as well. The brochure promised every modern amenity."

"Spiffing," said Tufty, and set off in search of them.

Left to himself, Jack had to admit that the Bay Sands Hotel was impressive. The long sleek curve of the building soared upwards like the side of an ocean liner, moored alongside the bay road. It was squared-off at the aft end towards the town, belled out towards him and was sharply pointed at the bows. A guest in one of those forward rooms would have a grandstand view of the jetty, the golf course and the road.

Tilting his head backwards to look up, the similarity to a liner became even more marked with two rows of balconied windows giving the appearance of rectangular portholes. Above them, set back from a railed edge, roof-terrace suites rose like the bridge of a ship, the windows reflecting the blue-grey of the sky and the sea. Everything proclaimed the building's modernity. Even the drainpipes and ornamental bosses looking like the capitals of Doric columns had been painted white so as not to mar the facade. All in all, thought Jack, a lot of money had been expended on a new hotel in a town which had been gently decaying since its heyday some forty years ago. The investigative journalist who was his alter ego was itching to know why.

He turned, tipped the driver who was preparing to return to the station to meet the next train, picked up his own suitcases and braced himself for a week of pleasure.

The large, curved cocktail terrace encircled the square end of the building, but the area immediately in front of the Bay Sands Hotel was unadorned save for low walls punctuated by benches. Wide triangles of turned earth on each side indicated the future presence of flower beds. The entrance was as modern as the rest, a handsome glass conservatory flanked by full-height Doric columns and filled with a variety of hot-house plants. Jack, who had stayed in continental resorts where similar plants grew like weeds in the grounds, admitted the result to be pleasing. The grand reception hall had plush maroon carpets, deep armchairs and a curving staircase to the floors above. The manager of the hotel himself greeted each guest and gave them their key. A line of bell boys stood waiting to take charge of the luggage and conduct the guests to their rooms.

Jack wondered if this was normal procedure or whether Mr Fauntleroy Delaney - he checked the nameplate on the desk again - whether Mr Fauntleroy Delaney was appearing in person today because this was the week of the official launch celebration for the Bay Sands Hotel.

"You've been open for some time, I believe," he said, signing the register and glancing over a number of names he recognised. Thalia Portman's signature sprawled across several lines. He hoped her bell boy was made of stern stuff.

"Yes indeed, sir," said Mr Delaney. "It is always advisable to postpone the official celebrations by a few months to ensure everything is running smoothly."

"Good show. Incidentally, my friend Mr Bridgewater has been delayed and will not be arriving until tomorrow."

"Very well, sir. I trust you will both enjoy your stay."

"I can't see why we wouldn't. It all looks splendid," said Jack and asked the lad who carried his case to room 17 how he liked working in the resort's newest hotel.

The boy replied obediently that he liked it very much, just like a home from home it was, except everyone was more polite and there was better grub.

A tip having been pocketed, the bedroom door was closed. Jack winced at the swirling blues and greys of the furnishings and went out to the balcony where he rested his arms comfortably on the chest-high rail and stared first across the wide sandy bay towards the sea, and then along the coast road which skirted the golf course and wound through scattered villages towards the rather brighter lights of Skegness. He wasn't quite at the prow of the building, but he'd been right about the magnificent view. In the corner room next to him, the balcony door also opened. With a sense of inevitability, Jack saw Phoebe Sugar step through it.

CHAPTER TWO

"We meet again," he said.

She looked across, her eyes gleaming with unmistakable invitation. "So we do. Your room or mine?"

Jack vaulted lightly over the wrought-iron divider and drew her inside.

"I'd heard you were a fast worker," she murmured.

He kissed her. It felt remarkably good. "Lucy, you minx. I thought you weren't going to make it to the station before the hotel charabanc left."

She gave him the sparkling, impish look he loved. "I nearly didn't. The head housekeeper made me do one of my bathrooms again. I had to beg a lift on the back of the saxophonist's motorcycle. Fortunately he's always happy to go for a spin with no questions asked. We arrived just as the train drew in, then I needed to dash around to the ladies to change." She wriggled out of his embrace, removed her blonde wig carefully, extracted her own handbag from Phoebe's bag, then delved further down and started hanging up the clothes she wore as Phoebe. "It's so nice to have somewhere to keep stuff again. My room in the staff block is tiny. Thank you for bringing the bag. I hope the creases fall out before I need to dress. Phoebe has very strict standards."

Jack watched her fondly. "Did you choose this bedroom especially?" He was in no doubt she would have done. The decor was more restful than his for a start.

"Myrtle in the office allocates the rooms. I said Phoebe was one of the writers for 'Society Snippets' in the *Chronicle* and she'd better put her somewhere nice. I also suggested that if it was one of the rooms I serviced, I could make sure everything was extra lovely so she'd give the hotel a good write-up. Myrtle is Mr Delaney's niece, so she agreed. Horribly exploited, poor lamb, but doesn't realise it."

Jack had every expectation that Myrtle would cease to be horribly exploited before Lucy left. "You've told me about her. She adds up columns of figures in her head, her brother is an apprentice at the garage by the golf course and when you went to tea with her, her mother never stopped talking. How did you get me and Charles next door?"

"I said I remembered reading in an article that Phoebe had a thing for you. Myrtle said she didn't blame her."

"It's more the other way about," said Jack and captured her hands. "Leave that. I've missed you."

"I've missed you too. Writing letters every day isn't the same as seeing you, and using the phone booth in the garage gets expensive. This investigation for your uncle better be worth it. Of all the boring jobs, being a chambermaid takes the biscuit. It's even worse than working as a nippie in a Corner House."

Jack grinned. His uncle was Curtis of the Yard, currently curious as to why persons of considerable financial acumen should be interested in owning a loss-making luxury hotel on an undeveloped stretch of the east coast. Quite apart from gathering information on their own account, Jack and Lucy were his unofficial eyes and ears. "I'll pass that on," he said. "I'm sure he'll be devastated."

Lucy chuckled. "I'll bet. What kept you? I've been here three weeks. There is very little about the daily routine of the Bay Sands Hotel I don't know by now. It is monotonously conventional and Myrtle looks after the accounts so I honestly doubt there is any financial hanky panky. However, it cannot be a coincidence that a great many of the staff are Russian."

"So you wrote, which is why Charles is joining us. I can't see a connection myself, but he may be able to make sense of it. He'll be here tomorrow."

"Can Charles speak Russian then?"

"He speaks everything. At school he used to take the French and Latin lessons if the master was indisposed. With his brain, he ought to be running the country, but he says it would be tedious."

"I hope he makes more progress with the staff than I've managed. I have asked why there are so many of them here, but they just shrug and smile and say it is good to be with other Russians."

"You didn't tell me you could speak Russian. I needn't have dragged Charles up here after all."

"I can't. Not really," said Lucy. "There was a White Russian army training camp in Newmarket during the last year of the war. They were shipped over from prisoner of war compounds in Germany after the revolution. The conditions they were kept in overseas was terrible and they were simply turned out after Russia signed the pact with Germany. Some of the officers needed medical attention so were admitted to our hospital. I've never seen men so thin. I picked up a few phrases while I was nursing them. Not enough for a proper conversation."

"So much I don't know about you. I remember the officer training now. The government were even more worried about the Bolsheviks than they were about the Boche. The takeover was doomed, of course. There weren't enough of them. The Red Army overran them in the second revolution, poor souls."

"My mother wrote recently saying two of the men I nursed have come back with their families to work with the horses. They like it better here than Russia because there is food and the English are kind. My father isn't bothered where his stable hands come from as long as they are good workers."

"I can see his point. To get back to *our* point which is why the grand opening was put off, I was hoping you might have an idea. We certainly don't."

"All I know is that the staff were called into the lounge and given a pep talk by Mr Delaney, thanking us for getting the place looking so marvellous and telling us not to rest on our laurels. He then rambled on about plans having changed and said we'd be hosting a home-refrigeration manufacturing symposium for a few days and then we could have the launch."

"Just that?"

"He also said there was nothing wrong with refrigerators and they were jolly useful for a lot of people and in the future every home would have one."

Jack grinned, but said thoughtfully, "Veronique Carter has been out of circulation for a week or so. Her father is one of the consortium that own the hotel. If the launch was delayed because of Veronique being unable to travel, it could indicate Mr Carter wants to transact some business with one of the other guests while they are here."

"Miss Carter seems fighting fit now. They arrived yesterday, complete with his valet and her maid. They've booked two of the roof-terrace suites. Myrtle says they always have the two at the prow of the building because Mr Carter's sitting room has a large table where he can keep up with his work. It was designed especially for him. They were here a lot while the hotel was being fitted out.

The top floor suites were the first to be fixed up for that reason. Evidently you don't get to be a tobacco tycoon by sneaking away on holiday whenever you feel like it. He's also brought two secretaries with him, would you believe."

"He always does," said Jack. "They were on the Atlantic crossing with us. Clean-cut, efficient young men with as much conversation as a pair of oysters."

"I'm guessing it's not a coincidence that Mr Carter keeps popping up in your investigations."

"I told my uncle you were smart. No, it isn't a coincidence. Self-made men, however rich they are, can never resist the opportunity to make a bit more. The question is whether those opportunities are on the level. Everything Edward Carter does is of interest, whether it is crossing the Atlantic for no discernable reason or sinking money in new hotels. Unfortunately Scotland Yard can't detail resources to check him out without reasonable grounds."

"Well, he must be planning a lot of business if the hotel has put off a whole swanky party until he could get here. Not to mention causing Mr Delaney to perjure his immortal soul by being nice to appliance manufacturers."

"One assumes the refrigerator men paid the going rate, which would have eased the pain. How did he get them here at such short notice?"

"Outbreak of food poisoning at the Resplendent. According to Myrtle, hotels often have an agreement between each other to help out in emergencies. She used to work for Mr Delaney at his previous hotel in Kentish Town before it was knocked down to build a cigarette factory, so she knows the form. She says the Bay Sands is far grander with a much better clientele."

"I can believe that."

"It is odd though, Jack. There's plenty going on at the hotel to keep people occupied, but the rest of Kingsthorpe is all lacy teashops and faded boarding houses. New shops are starting to emerge from old ones, a refurbished art gallery is opening on the town quay next week, there's talk of a pier, the garage along the road has got a modern workshop, space for hotel guests to keep cars and quarters for their chauffeurs, but all these things are just pinpricks. A few brilliants in a sea of tired paste. It really doesn't say smart set to me."

"Cause and effect, maybe. New hotel, new opportunities. These things take time."

"They must have been confident it would work. Irene is a local girl and she says the feeling in the town originally was that the hotel would be a white elephant. Mind you, she also says the majority of the residents wouldn't know a money-spinner if it exploded five pound notes all over them. According to her, Kingsthorpe is the fustiest place on the coast. There was a brief flurry of alarm when so many Russians started appearing around the town, but they are very quiet and have such nice manners that they are simply accepted now, particularly as some have moved into the most run-down properties and are cheerfully renovating them."

"How enlightened of the townsfolk. Not even any cautionary Little-Russia-By-The-Sea articles in the local paper?"

"The *Kingsthorpe Enquirer* only has one reporter plus a lady who does the funerals and weddings. Irene says people mainly buy it for the picture house listings and the For Sale column."

Jack was affronted. "Shocking. Local papers should be the life-blood of the community."

"Not in Kingsthorpe. Personally, I hope the hotel owners being here this week will be the catalyst for something happening. The excitement of making endless beds and cleaning acres of enamel and chrome wore off some time ago."

"You mean you haven't got an idea for a future book out of it yet?" he teased.

Lucy gave him an old-fashioned look. "I've got ideas for several books. It *is* supposed to be why I'm here if I'm rumbled. I'd quite like to get back to London now to write them."

He grinned at her. As well as sporadically reporting for the society pages as Phoebe Sugar, Lucy wrote detective novels as Leonora Benson and career-girl adventure books as Lois Barrabell. They brought her in a respectable income, if only - as she complained - she didn't have to keep interrupting the flow of ideas with the need to go out to work to get the requisite background research. "Go on, then," he said, "what are these new books going to be called?"

"*Hetty Hargraves: Hotelier* for clean-living career-minded girls. That's going to be as dull as ditch-water. I'm thinking of calling the other one *Murder in the Palm Court Lounge* and have the victim found by the cleaners first thing in the morning face down in the ornamental fountain."

"Nice," said Jack appreciatively.

"I thought so. You wait until you see the thing, it's a menace. My real difficulty is staying awake long enough to write anything. I'm jotting down hotel notes as I think of them, otherwise I've just about managed to finish the first draft of *The Dead Man at Table 13* and that's it. Chamber-maiding is very physically demanding, let me tell you."

"So is being inoffensively affable to wealthy businessmen, which is what I seem to have been doing solidly for a fortnight. Who killed your man at table 13? That's the Lyons corner house book, isn't it?"

"Yes, using my nippie experience. It was one of the under-chefs. He used to be in service until he was sacked for carrying on with his master's mistress. He hated the fact that he'd been reduced to working in a common café due to not having references. He recognised the victim as his former employer because of his finicky elevenses order. The gentleman always wanted blackcurrant jam, not blackberry jam, with the pat of butter on the side of the toast."

"Good lord. Did nobody see him do it?"

"No, he took off his chef's whites and hid a knife under his jacket. Slid the knife into his ex-master, went back though the staff door and carried on chopping up mutton for the daily special."

"Remind me never to eat in a Lyons again. To business. Tell me about the hotel set-up, then we can get on with something more interesting."

"Goodness, Mr Sinclair, whatever can you mean?"

"Give me the low down on the layout and I'll show you."

"I've told you all about it in my letters."

"Yes, but it's different now I'm here. Besides, I like listening to you and watching you talk. I've missed that."

"Six foot of solid charm, that's you. All right then. The ground floor is where all the public areas are. That's the dining room, lounge, bar, casino, various sitting rooms, card rooms, billiard room, beauty suite. The casino is a huge draw. A party from Skegness came up in three cars last week and spent the whole evening spending money in it. I've never seen Mr Delaney so happy."

"I imagine he will be ecstatic this week, then. Is it on the level?"

"It's licenced, so I assume so. To continue, also on the ground floor, the kitchen, laundry and staff quarters are squashed into the short wing of the pointed bit next to the gardens. The Russians who live-in have their own accommodation block further back."

"Squashed? Really? The building looks so impressive."

"All hotels are alike, according to Irene. You should hear her on the subject of staff conditions at the Savoy in London. At least we have it better here than she did there. The Bay Sands Hotel is sleek at the front where it shows, and stepped at the back where it doesn't matter. Pyotr, who is one of the gardeners, shakes his head portentously whenever he looks at all the flat bits of roof and says there will be trouble with leaks once the rains start. He gave me a ten minute lecture in Russian, with hand gestures, about the correct pitch and angle of roof tiles. I couldn't understand one word in twenty, but the mime was crystal clear. Honestly, if the training didn't take six years, I'd be tempted to write *Anna Adams: Architect* next."

"Alongside *The Gable End Murders,* no doubt. It's an idea. You could probably pick up enough lingo by getting a temporary job in the office of a architect practice. How is your shorthand?"

She wrinkled her nose. "It needs a refresher course."

"Oh well. Where were we?"

"Stop that. I was telling you about the hotel. There are twenty-four bedrooms on the first floor, handily numbered 1-24. I service these front twelve with the balconies, the twelve at the back share bathrooms and don't have balconies. They are cheaper, of course."

"Makes sense."

Lucy nodded. "Except even the cheaper ones aren't that cheap. They look out over the gardens and the tennis courts. The second floor is narrower, with only twelve rooms (numbered 25-36), all with balconies and a bay or golf-course view. Then there are eight suites on the top floor (numbered 37-44), set back with roof terraces at the front instead of balconies. Those are really expensive."

"I don't suppose you know who is in them this week?"

"The Carters have their two suites. Mr & Mrs Mackenzie have another one, and there is also a Mr

Forrest. Myrtle says they've all been several times before, including when it was still being fitted out."

Jack nodded. "Mackenzie and Forrest are part of the consortium. Mackenzie runs a large construction empire and Forrest is a banker. They are both longtime associates of Edward Carter. I've met them all in London recently. It makes sense that they'd be at the Bay Sands Hotel for the grand opening, but any business meetings could be carried out just as easily in the city as they could here."

Lucy shrugged. "There is also Gustav Karlsson, who is a regular guest and who is Swedish. Myrtle says he owns two merchant ships with plans for more, has a house in Lysekil on the Swedish west coast, is kind to his mother, has lovely eyes and looks like Douglas Fairbanks Jr."

"Is Myrtle a little smitten, do we think?"

"I can't say I've noticed."

Jack chuckled. "He's not one of the owners, but he'll bear watching if he's a regular here. Will there be anyone this week who knows you?"

"Only you and Charles. Some of the guests have horses with my father, but they won't recognise me as I'm rarely at home these days. I've written about a number of the visitors for 'Society Snippets' before now. Most won't give me a second glance, but I did persuade Myrtle to put the Lester family in two rooms on the second floor to be on the safe side. I don't think even Julie and Amanda could fail to notice a resemblance if I was taking their photographs as Phoebe in the Palm Court lounge at night and cleaning their bathroom as Lucy next morning."

"I wouldn't be so sure," said Jack dubiously. "However, their mother certainly would. Your eyes are quite distinctive and not much gets past Mrs Lester."

Lucy unfolded a sheet of paper from her handbag. "These are the guests I've found out about so far, all the ones on this floor and a few higher up. It's tricky getting a sight of the bookings. I'll need to distract Myrtle for the rest if you want them."

"It could be handy." He scanned the list. "A lot of the usual crowd, I see. Thank goodness Thalia Portman isn't on this floor. I'd defy even Mr Carter's secretary-oysters to avoid her." He stopped at one of the names, honestly astonished. "Well now, that *is* interesting."

"What is?"

He tapped the list. "This chap here. Xavier Hilliard. He's the last man I would expect to see at a resort hotel. It's not often he ventures out from the capital."

"Why?"

"Largely because he is too busy tending his web. He specialises in, shall we say, obliging the susceptible with loans until quarter day arrives. Top notch clients. Very discreet. Large sums not a problem providing you can lay your hands on a mortgage for him to look after as security."

"Nice chap."

"Not especially. He came from nowhere some years ago. All of a sudden there he was, with an office in Harley Street just like a society doctor. Unlike a society doctor, there have been quite a number of suicides amongst his clients. Scotland Yard have been unable to touch him, no matter how hard they dig. It's surprisingly difficult to research his past, which is suspicious enough. One source claims he is the illegitimate son of deposed royalty, another has him escaping from an Eastern European circus, yet another maintains he is the offspring of a cabaret dancer and a visiting seaman."

"Smokescreen? The name Hilliard doesn't sound particularly exotic."

"No. Wherever he came from, he evidently applied himself to the English language before reinventing Xavier Hilliard as a helpful denizen of the financial scene. I would love to get a story on him. There's got to be one if he's here."

"This may be your opportunity."

"Wouldn't that be a bonus. Good lord, Jimmy Ward has booked too, sharing with Tufty Thomas. This place must be making a name for itself."

"That's what Mr Delaney keeps telling us. He says people will be calling Kingsthorpe the East Coast Riviera before the season is over."

"Evidently an optimistic type. Talking of optimism, have you got anything else to tell me and is anyone likely to interrupt us for a while?"

She chuckled. "Probably, but my mind has gone blank, and no, we won't be interrupted in this room. I locked the door after the bell boy and I happen to know the chambermaid is out on the dunes this afternoon writing dutiful letters home. Annoyingly, she has to be back at six for an hour to do a circuit of the whole floor with clean towels in case any of the guests have been inconsiderate enough to bathe before dinner."

"Good for her," said Jack. He bolted the balcony window and drew the curtains. "Any more intelligence gathering for Uncle Bob can wait until tea. Have you any idea how long three weeks apart is when I'd only just found you again in the first place?"

"Now you come to mention it, yes," said Lucy, and moved into his arms.

CHAPTER THREE

Afternoon tea was taken in the Palm Court lounge. A pianist played gently in one corner, vying with the supposedly soothing patter of water droplets from the ornamental fountain just inside the doorway. Lucy could only assume the designer who had sold the owners the idea of a fountain had never had to live with one. She'd already learnt to give it a wide berth to avoid getting her clothes wet and she was hardly ever in here.

Aside from the fountain, the lounge was looking a good deal gayer than when it was hosting the refrigeration symposium. The bright hues of the latest fashion made a welcome change from business suits. There was also a lot of lively conversation as many of the visitors knew each other. As Jack had once told her, the wealthy set roamed around the smart places of the continent as a loose pack, breaking off into eddies to this watering place or that casino, then coming together again for the big race meetings, the fashion shows, the charity galas. They were like the sea washing over an expanse of tidal pools, constantly ebbing and flowing and reforming.

Today bore that out. There were cries of recognition from groups of guests, delicate embraces, tables moved together by waiters so the newly reunited could sit together.

Lucy was wasting no time in establishing Phoebe's credentials. She hadn't missed Mr Delaney's momentary check when she'd collected her key. He might well wonder why a gossip columnist rated a luxe room with a bay view rather than a rear single with a shared bathroom, overlooking the tennis courts. Now she placed herself in his field of vision, taking a photo of two society matrons against a backdrop of geometric bone china teacups and a tiered cake stand. That should mollify him.

She moved on with a lingering regret for the tiny sandwiches and the cakes. It seemed to have been a long while since lunch and she wouldn't be able to have the early dinner in the staff block. Being two people was awfully time-consuming.

On the other side of the lounge, a gentleman she didn't recognise rose in an aggressive manner and came over to her. "I don't care for my photograph being taken," he said. "Not in any shots, not single or groups. Got that?"

"Certainly," said Lucy.

"Remember it."

Other people tip me for favours. The thought was in her mind, but Lucy said nothing. She did, however, make a mental note to ask Jack who he was. Before she could do so there was a stir in the doorway. Veronique Carter - the sole heiress to a tobacco industry fortune - stood there in a deceptively simple scarlet day dress with half-a-dozen ropes of graduated pearls dropping to her waist, her father a watchful presence at her shoulder.

Her arrival was the signal for a number of young men to leap to their feet. Jack, Lucy was glad to see, stood in a more leisurely fashion. Lucy herself, motivated by something that was probably a mean desire not to have the male complement of the Palm Court lounge fall at Miss Carter's feet, got there first.

"Phoebe Sugar. 'Society Snippets' in *The Chronicle*," she

murmured. "Just a quick photograph for our readers, then I won't intrude on the remainder of your afternoon. Adore the dress. Vionnet, is it?"

Veronique took up a pose next to the fountain without even thinking about it. "It is. You have quite an eye, Miss Sugar."

Lucy lined up for the shot, just as her mentor had taught her when she was researching *Death on the Catwalk.* "Quality always tells, Miss Carter," she said respectfully, and clicked the shutter on Veronique's lifted chin and satisfied smile. It would be a good photo, lovely angles and shadows. She hadn't even had to warn her about the spray from the fountain. There was no point alienating the very people who contributed to a useful sideline income. She continued to work her way around the room.

"Who is the tall, heavyset gentleman in the brown suit with the fawn tie?" she murmured as she passed Jack some fifteen minutes later. "Over there talking to Gina Bianca, the actress."

"I don't know." There was mild astonishment in his voice at this gap in his knowledge. "Not one of the normal crowd. I don't even know his face. Bodyguard, maybe. He's protective enough."

Lucy frowned down at her camera, her lips barely moving. "That might explain why he doesn't want to be photographed. He told me so in no uncertain terms."

"Interesting. Can you take a shot anyway? I can send it to Uncle Bob."

"Not in these clothes or with this camera. I'm too noticeable. I might be able to get one as Lucy with my little Kodak if he goes outside for a walk or to play tennis. Drat, I need a new roll of film. See you later."

She raised her head, gave Jack a social smile as if they'd been discussing the weather and moved on, pausing to allow a group she recognised through the doorway.

Predictably, there were squeals from the two young women in their skimpy summer-resort frocks, as they came within range of the fountain.

And then more squeals as they in turn recognised *her*. "Oh! You're Phoebe Sugar!" exclaimed Julie Lester. "You were on the Atlantic crossing when we both got engaged. You took that dreamy photograph of us that was in the *New York Evening Post*. And it was in 'Society Snippets' when we got back home."

Her twin smiled at Lucy in a friendly fashion. "Our housekeeper keeps a cuttings book. Are you here for the grand opening?"

"*The Chronicle* likes to keep up to date with the newest happenings," said Lucy obliquely. "Any advance notice of when the weddings are to be? I won't tell a soul."

The Lester twins giggled at this patent untruth. "Secret," said Amanda. "But we'll send you an invitation. Have you got a card? I'll give it to Mummy. She organises us. We just have the fun."

Lucy gave her one of Phoebe's cards. The address was the smallest bed-sitting room in the same building as Lucy's flat. It had frequently proved useful. "I'm just going to fetch a new roll of film, then I'll be down to take your photographs. Are your fiancés here?"

"Couldn't get in, poor poppets. They're at the Resplendent. They'll be joining us for dinner. Do move, Amanda, I'm getting soaked by this silly fountain."

As Lucy crossed the reception hall towards the stairs, she felt cautiously pleased. The conversation had been well within Mr Delaney's hearing, and seeing her greeted with delight by the Lesters must now make him consider her having one of the nicest first-floor rooms a publicity investment.

Lucy's shoes made no noise on the dense pile of the corridor carpet. Conversation, laughter and the chink of tea cups floated up from downstairs, but otherwise she might have been alone. The click of her key in the lock sounded preternaturally loud. It was answered by the tiniest echo.

Lucy stopped. She might only have booked in as Phoebe Sugar today, but she had been cleaning this room for three weeks and she knew there was someone else in here. The curtains she had left open were now drawn. They stirred in the draught from the balcony door. The same door that she had shut and bolted behind Jack earlier.

It didn't occur to her that dashing across the room and whipping the curtains open was a stupid thing to do. Fortunately for her - as Jack made quite plain later - there was no one outside. She looked along the length of the balconies to the far end. There was no one there either. She couldn't see around the corner at this end. The line of balconies ended at hers and restarted with the first room on the short wing facing the golf course. Lucy bolted the balcony door, snatched a new roll of film from her drawer and went downstairs to make a fuss.

"There was *what*?"

"Keep your voice down." As Phoebe, she was partaking of her belated tea in the Palm Court lounge. Nothing had ever tasted quite so good.

Jack had dropped into the chair next to her, doing his best impression of an idle playboy, flirting with a pretty woman to pass the time. He lifted his hand to the waiter to bring another cup. "Repeat what you just said?"

"There was someone in my room. They escaped via the balcony."

"Was anything taken? Disturbed?"

"Not that I could see, but I'll have to make doubly sure I remember to lock Phoebe's wig away when I'm being Lucy. Can you keep my rolls of film in your strongbox?"

"Of course." Jack smiled beguilingly at her for the benefit of any onlookers. "What did the manager say? I noticed you having artistically agitated words with him but I wasn't close enough to the doorway to hear you."

"He was shocked. Appalled. Never in any hotel under his direction etc etc."

"Naturally not. Why are you being so calm about this?"

Lucy ate a cherry-and-almond slice thoughtfully. "Largely because Mr Delaney was very concerned that the experience might have given me a dislike of the room and asked whether I would like to change to a different one."

"Interesting."

"Especially as the hotel is fully booked." She paused. "It might be something, Jack. I don't know whether I imagined it, but I got the impression when I arrived that he wasn't expecting Phoebe Sugar to be in that particular room. There was a hesitation before he selected the key. When I'm Lucy again tomorrow, I might drop in on Myrtle to see how she is bearing up under the strain of a full house."

"Take care. We don't want anyone noticing that both Lucy and Phoebe have the finest pair of light green eyes in the country."

Lucy beat down a flicker of gratification. "Hush. Myrtle stays in her office and never sees the guests as a rule, so she is safe enough. Mr Delaney has nothing to do with the upstairs staff and if he does ever come upon me when I'm chatting to Myrtle, I keep my eyes lowered and scuttle away fast. As for the guests, one chambermaid looks much like another to them. All they notice is the mob cap and the washed-out blue of the uniform. The only person I'll have to be careful about is Irene. She'd know me."

"Can she get into your room?"

"Of course she can. We are chambermaids, Jack, we have pass keys. We can get into all the rooms."

"I don't like it."

"That makes two of us. However, if anyone does tumble to my dual personality, it won't matter too much. As Lucy, I'm researching the next Leonora Benson book, which my publisher already knows about in case verification is needed. As for Phoebe, I'll say the job came up, it's only for a few days and I wasn't going to turn down the extra pay. I'm trusting your uncle to have covered the tracks at the *Chronicle* end."

Jack sighed. "I'm all for equality in life, but sometimes it worries me that you are the exact partner-in-crime Uncle Bob would have picked for me if he'd had any say in the matter."

Lucy grinned at him unrepentantly and bit into a delicate, melting pastry confection to mask it. "Which he didn't. We picked each other."

"You can't deny he welcomed you with open arms as soon as I introduced you. As any man of sense would," he added hastily.

"Nice recovery. Haven't you been sitting here rather a long time?"

Jack drained his tea and stood up. "Cruel creature. I daresay we shall meet again after dinner. Will there be dancing?"

"Certainly. Let me know who you would like me to take a photo of you with."

He sketched her a jaunty salute and crossed the room.

From his position behind the long, burr-walnut reception counter, Fauntleroy Delaney had a commanding view of his empire. Behind him he could hear the whisper of his assistant's pencil and the muted industry of the young woman on the telephone switchboard. Myrtle was busy in her office. His own snug domain waited in readiness for when he needed to talk privately to a client. He gazed with swelling heart at the glass entrance doors, the lush conservatory, the lift to the upper floors, the stairs, the invitingly open door to the bar, the currently closed doors to the casino and dining room, and the gilded, Egyptian-style archway to the Palm Court lounge. It was all he'd ever wanted from life.

A sliver of disquiet pierced his pleasure. It was through the Egyptian archway that Miss Sugar had gone, understandably agitated, in search of tea. Delaney had seen her earlier taking a photograph of Miss Carter. He had heard her in laughing conversation with the wealthy Lester twins. None of this would do his hotel any harm. He hoped he had been soothing enough regarding the intruder she swore had been on her balcony, so that she wouldn't mention the incident in her column. All the same, he could wish she wasn't in that particular room. Murmuring to his assistant to take his place at the counter, he went through to his niece's office.

Myrtle, pale blonde hair pulled back into a messy bun, inkstained fingers marking her place in the staff wages ledger, was writing a note on her pad. Delaney tutted under his breath. A good girl, serious and conscientious like her mother. He wouldn't be able to run the hotel without her, but there was no denying she was not presentable enough to have anywhere near the guests.

"Myrtle," he said.

"Hello, Uncle Faun. There's a message just come in by telephone from Immingham for Mr Karlsson. I'm writing it down ready for when he arrives. Is it nearly time for tea? I'm parched."

"Yes, they should be bringing it along. Put the message in Mr Karlsson's pigeon hole. He's in his usual suite, I take it?"

"Oh yes, I made sure of that." She blushed a faint pink which gave her quite a nice colour.

"Talking of the bookings, the guest in room 19. I thought one of the other visitors had requested it?"

Myrtle looked at him anxiously. "Not specifically. Miss Bianca wanted a corner balcony so she would have the bay as a backdrop in her publicity photos. I gave her 25 as it's nice and high. Someone else asked for a corner room with a bay view, so I gave him room 1. Wasn't that right?"

So much for his unwelcome guest saying he had written with explicit instructions. "That must be what I remembered. I should have known you would have dealt with everything. This Phoebe Sugar, what are her columns like? Will she be good publicity for us?"

"Golly, yes," said Myrtle with enthusiasm. "Haven't you read any? 'Society Snippets' in the *Chronicle* is ever so popular. Uncle, another of the musicians has left. That's two this week as well as a waiter going last week. I don't understand. Why do people keep leaving? Why don't they like it here?"

"The sea air doesn't agree with everyone."

"But that's not the case with Yuri, because I saw him in town with his wife. He said they have settled nicely."

"Perhaps the work was too hard. Yuri is not a young man. His son is still with us."

Myrtle's mouth opened as if she was going to fret some more, so he cut in quickly.

"Never mind about the musician. They are a breed apart. The safety of a steady income and a roof over their heads unnerves them. If he asks for a reference refer it to me. You'd better run an advert for a replacement."

Myrtle made an obedient note. Delaney left the office to perambulate in a stately fashion amongst his guests. He stopped a waiter and reminded him to take a tray of tea and some of the fancy cakes through to Myrtle. He knew from past experience that a sweet treat had the unfailing effect of distracting his niece's mind from any speculation about his conversation.

Back at his command post, he glanced at the board of keys. Several guests had not yet arrived. When they did, his hotel would be full - with no chance of moving guests out of rooms on spurious excuses. The bar trade would be brisk, the roulette wheels would click, the beach would be gay with water sports and the Palm Court lounge would be a tapestry of elegant clothes and refined conversation. And these guests would tell their smart friends and those friends would tell others and next year they might need to build a hotel annexe on part of the golf course. Delaney sent his assistant to tea and slipped effortlessly into his favourite daydream.

Dinner was useful more for assessing who was present than for the amassing of information. It was, as Jack had already established, a familiar crowd. People wanting to be seen in the latest smart place, people looking for the twin drugs of fun and distraction, people with money to spend and nothing to fill their days. It was a milieu he moved in out of necessity and was increasingly disillusioned with.

It was all so empty, so devoid of purpose. It was as if the nine years since the end of the war had anaesthetised people's moral compass. Not so, himself. All the heady amusement in the world couldn't make him forget that horrific period, the friends he had lost, the terrible waste.

That was the obverse side to those war years. The sense of being spared for a reason, the guilt that better men than him had died while he had lived, these were enough to drive Jack to do something worthwhile with his life, to make a difference. It was a grim irony that to succeed, he had to appear as idle and carefree as those around him.

He turned his mind to the Bay Sands Hotel. Why was it here in this place? What was the consortium's underlying purpose? Not for one moment did Jack think they had built it out of mere speculation.

He did notice the prevalence of Russian waiters. A watchful, compact senior man seemed to combine his own duties with the smoothing out of queries, throwing in a spot of translation for good measure. He might bear closer observation.

Throughout the meal, Jack was aware, half the dining room away, of Phoebe Sugar conversing with her table companions. Lucy had evidently done her chambermaid act with the towels after tea and then metamorphosed back to Phoebe while he was in the bar listening to Mr Mackenzie discourse about the building opportunities available for new businesses when this part of the coast took off as a high-class resort. *When,* Jack noted, not *if.* Mrs Mackenzie had drily voiced the opinion that fancy piers were all very well, but if one of those business could be a fashionable dress shop and another sold hats belonging in this century rather than the previous one, it would be a good start.

Jack had worried how Lucy would manage the social part of the assignment. Phoebe Sugar was a fabrication, designed to flit into a theatre foyer or nightclub or garden party, take a few photographs, and then sell them (accompanied by some well chosen words) to 'Society Snippets' or whoever else had given her a commission. Was she having to create Phoebe a personality? A history? It shouldn't be beyond her capabilities, being a writer, so long as she remembered everything she invented.

Having several personae himself, Jack was surprised at how conflicted he felt about Lucy playing a part so publicly. Not so much at her chambermaid duties because as she'd said, people rarely saw beyond the uniform, but society reporters inhabited his own spectrum. The two of them hadn't been together long enough to be viewed as a couple and whilst Jack could see that the current situation suited his uncle very well, not acknowledging

Lucy as herself in public was already beginning to chafe on him. Would his circle of acquaintance recognise her as Phoebe when their relationship became known? Perhaps they might think he simply had a predilection for young women with light green eyes.

A voice from his own table recalled him. "Not seen you recently, Jack. Where have you been? We heard you picked a fight with a cab in New York."

"Yes, I don't advise it," said Jack ruefully. "I wasn't concentrating. Forgot the traffic was back to front on the other side of the Atlantic. Fortunately I bounced. My mother always says I'm made from indiarubber. Where did you go after New York?"

Theo Nicholson cut into his steak with gusto. "Grub's good here, isn't it? Where did we go? Cannes, wasn't it, Hubert? Then toured along the coast with the girls, then London and now up here. To be frank, I could do with rather more settling down and not so much tootling about, but Ma-in-law-to-be has set her heart on a double autumn wedding, so as she's the one paying..."

"Sickening for you. Do I gather you couldn't get rooms here? What's the Resplendent like?"

"Cheaper," said Hubert, dropping his voice so the others didn't hear. "Suits us. You must come down and blow a cloud."

"I'll do that. Charles is arriving tomorrow. I'll drag him out for a walk along the bay towards town. It'll do him good."

"Somebody was saying he'd got a job, is that right? Foreign Office or such like. Doesn't sound much like Charles."

Jack gave an easy chuckle. "Oh, that. It's hardly onerous. It's not even a real job. He's obliging his godfather by doing the pretty to visiting bigwigs. I rather think some settling of his tailor's bills may have been involved in return. You have to admit he has the right manner for it. The Italian ambassador's wife thought he was one of the royal cousins and was asking all sorts of questions about the internal workings of Buckingham Palace. I dread to think what he told her."

In truth, Charles's semi-diplomatic post was no more real than Jack's playboy image, both were cover for their real work and both those occupations were clandestine for different reasons. Jack's hard-hitting articles about the underbelly of society would make his present life untenable if he was known to be the journalist Jonathan Curtis. As for Charles, the knowledge that he was employed by the Naval Intelligence Division of the Admiralty was unlikely to be well received at a coastal resort hotel employing more than the average number of Russian émigrés.

CHAPTER FOUR

From the dining room, the guests dispersed to the casino, card rooms, bar or lounge, where the dance floor had been cleared of tables. Lucy passed quite close to the orchestra and was amused that the saxophonist didn't give her a second glance, despite her having ridden pillion on his motorcycle to the station earlier. As she had previously had occasion to notice, when she was Phoebe people only saw the pink and silver of her flapper dress, the silver bandeau around the blonde wig, the white or silver court shoes. All as far from Lucy's dark-haired, boxy blue and green image as possible. As an added precaution, she was intending to even scrub off Phoebe's fragrance with carbolic whenever she made the change.

She looked for Mr No Photographs, but he wasn't in here. The actress he had been talking to, Gina Bianca (who despite her name had been described as an English Rose in the publicity material for every film Lucy had seen her in), was raptly dancing a tango with a good-looking, slim-hipped gentleman in faultless evening dress.

She took a photo of them, wondering who he was. He was of moderate height and moved like a dancing pro, but the Bay Sands Hotel already had a professional couple giving a classically scornful performance on the far side of the dance floor. Jack would know. Turning to see if he was anywhere near, she caught sight of Mrs Lester watching Gina Bianca with a stony expression on her face. A tiny shock ran through her. This was far from the affable, indulgent woman she was familiar with. What had Miss Bianca done to deserve such a look? Tried to steal away either Theo or Hubert, the viscounts she had worked so hard to secure for her daughters?

She mentioned the incident to Jack when he paused beside her to survey the scene. "Who is her partner?" she asked. Gina certainly attracted interesting gentlemen and she appeared mesmerised by this one.

A meditative note crept into Jack's voice. "That is Xavier Hilliard. Don't let his suave charm fool you. Word has it he's like a terrier with a rat as soon as he sniffs a potential opportunity for profit. He has to be here for a reason."

"And you intend to find out what it is?"

"I do."

Lucy felt a tiny ice-cold trickle along her spine. "You will be careful, won't you? He looks - I don't know - dangerous."

"I'm quite dangerous myself."

Was he? She supposed he must be. He'd never told her about the specific work he had done during the war. Their relationship had been so rapid, a lot was still unsaid. "It that was supposed to be reassuring, it failed," she replied tartly. "It still worries me that your accident in New York might have been a deliberate attempt to put you out of the way."

She knew by the stillness of his arm next to hers that he too believed it had been deliberate. He spoke with his customary lightness. "Which is why I'm pushing the amiable playboy act for all I'm worth and no longer coincidentally turning up in the vicinity of suspected drug-smuggling operations."

Lucy shivered. She dropped her voice still further. "And me? I went to that warehouse, Jack. You waited for me outside. What if they track me through you?"

He stared idly at the dancing couples. "Don't think I haven't considered that. When you *are* you, we will stay even further away from them. For now, you are Phoebe and in the eyes of the world, I have lost interest in children's playroom attendants."

And as Lucy, she had applied for this job using an address supplied by Chief Inspector Curtis. She breathed again, ashamed of her momentary weakness. There were hundreds of Lucy Browns in England, after all. "I take it back. It is reassuring to know you can be dangerous."

The music finished. Xavier Hilliard bowed to Gina Bianca and led her to a table. The actress sat down, giving her head a little shake as if she was trying to clear it, and reached for her glass. As Lucy watched, Xavier Hilliard (she found she believed in Xavier far more than she believed in Hilliard) strolled over to Veronique Carter and engaged her in conversation.

Jack gave a low whistle. "Edward Carter is not going to like that. He is still angling for the country's newest earl to pop the question to his beloved daughter."

Lucy snorted with derision. As if that was likely to matter where a personable man was concerned. Sure enough Veronique, who disliked not being the centre of attention and who had been following Gina Bianca's tango with narrowed eyes, smiled cooly and gave her hand to Mr Hilliard.

Elsewhere, the professional dancing couple finished their dance, separated, and took to the floor again with other partners. Having been ignored by her on the charabanc in favour of the driver, Lucy was not at all surprised to see Thalia Portman snagging the male dancer without any effort whatsoever.

"Do you know," said Jack. "I feel a sudden urge to cut Theo out and take Julie Lester for a twirl around the floor." He strolled off.

Left to herself, Lucy stifled the thought that she would also have quite liked to be taken for a twirl. She edged away from the dancers and wrote in her notebook who she'd taken photographs of so far. What she hadn't mentioned to Jack was that Xavier Hilliard was booked into one of the rooms she serviced. Judging by the way he was manoeuvring Julie Lester into the environs of Hilliard and Miss Carter, he might find that morsel of information of some interest.

To her horror, she felt a yawn creeping up on her and hurriedly swung around while she controlled it. This might be the only evening she would manage to mingle with the clientele. She was blowed if she was going to let a little thing like working a twenty-hour day cut it short. Where was a waiter with a tray of coffee when you needed one? A gust of male laughter halted her in her quest to find one. In the reception hall a large fair gentleman who had evidently just arrived was slapping Mr Delaney on the back. That was startling enough to chase any thoughts of tiredness away. Mr Delaney gestured towards the dining room, presumably asking the newcomer if he wanted something to eat.

The man nodded vigorously, tossed his overcoat and hat at a bell boy who staggered under the impact, and strode through the door, sweeping Mr Delaney along with him. Just before the dining room door swung shut, Lucy saw Grigory, assistant to the maitre d', hurry over wearing the closest thing to a smile she'd ever seen on his face.

"Well, well," said Lucy to herself. "Unless there are two guests this weekend with a striking resemblance to Douglas Fairbanks Jr, that was Mr Gustav Karlsson."

And on very matey terms with the management.

It was something else to tell Jack about. She returned thoughtfully to the lounge.

"Where are you going?" asked Jack sleepily.

"Work," said Lucy. "Staff breakfast is at five-thirty. I need to be in my quarters well beforehand in order to put on my uniform and come out for it. Go back to sleep. If you want to creep into your own room, do it discreetly. I'll find you either in here or in there at a more civilised hour."

Lucy tiptoed out, keeping a wary eye and ear open for the pre-dawn shoe cleaning team. As soon as she was safely out of doors, anyone spotting her would simply think she'd missed the last bus from town and had got a lift along the coast road with the mail van this morning rather than walk through the dark last night. Inside the hotel, there could be only one explanation for her presence in a bedroom corridor. Rather awkwardly, it would be correct.

All was quiet. Thank goodness for that. She hadn't intended staying this side of the hotel overnight, but the grounds had been full of revellers until late, and the temptation of a soft bed and Jack after three weeks apart had been too much. Resolving to do better for the rest of their stay, Lucy sped to the end of the corridor and ran lightly down the back stairs. She'd just laid her hand on the side door release, trying to ease the catch quietly, when she heard disembodied whispers above her in the stairwell.

"Just be sure you do."

"I've said so, haven't I? You stick to your part of the bargain and don't keep bothering me."

"I've said so, haven't I?" The savage mimicry sent a shiver through Lucy.

There was the sound of a door swinging to. She slipped

the side entrance catch in a panic and winged around the shadows of the path to the staff block, hardly breathing until she was safely in her room. Ten minutes later she was in nightclothes and dressing gown, splashing icy water over her face in the women's bathroom as if she'd just woken up.

"What a night," grumbled Irene as they queued for breakfast. "Did you hear those guests in the garden, partying until the small hours? Why couldn't they stay on the bar terrace? Inconsiderate, I call it. Never a thought for those of us who have to be awake first thing to look after them."

Lucy yawned. "I feel as if I'd only just shut my eyes," she agreed with some truth. "Did you have a good half-day?"

Irene shrugged. "Showed my face at home. Took May to the park to feed the ducks. Had a walk around the shops. It's looking up even more in town. A lot of the 'For Sale' boards have come down. There's a lovely jeweller, the bakery's changed hands and there's a new fancy goods shop opened where the stationer used to be. They've got some comical wooden animals in the window and of course May wanted one of the ducks. It should have been a shilling, but when we went in, it was Elsie Williams serving and I've known her for years. She said I could have this duck for sixpence because of it having a wonky leg. It's a foreign chap who makes them. He sits in the back room and carves and his wife makes the lacy mats. Elsie and the other girl don't have much to do with them. She said it's a good place if you like shop work." Irene sounded more cheerful as she related her afternoon.

"It's nice to have a catch up with a friend," said Lucy.

"Elsie's always been a good sort. A lot of them still cross the road when they see me coming in case my loose morals infect them. I saw a film in the evening with

Frank. He kept on at me to give up this job and get one at Woolworths like Gladys Perkins. I asked him when he last saw an opening advertised and said maybe he should be taking Gladys to the picture house if he was so keen on her prospects. I also reminded him I'm saving so I can move May and Ma down to Skegness where there's a bit more going on. He didn't like that. I wish he would take up with Gladys Perkins. He makes me tired, always putting me down."

"Perhaps he's worried one of the guests will fall madly in love with you and whisk you off to a life of unimagined luxury."

"I'm not stopping any of them."

Lucy grinned and they ate in a companionable silence before heading over to housekeeping to find out who was in, who was out and who wanted early tea in their rooms.

A soft tap at the bedroom door followed by the rattle of curtain rings informed Jack that the day had started.

"Your morning tea, sir," said a familiar voice. "You ordered it yesterday."

"Did I? How efficient of me." Jack opened his eyes with some reluctance, then sat bolt upright as he took in Lucy's muted, calf-length blue dress, complete with full apron and mob cap. "Cripes, I see what you mean. I hardly recognise you myself."

"Drink your nice tea and get dressed. The sooner you go down to breakfast, the sooner I can get on with cleaning your room. Your shoes have been polished. I've brought them in for you. All part of the Bay Sands Hotel service."

"Thank you. Leave them by the wardrobe and come here so I can make sure you are really you."

"No time for that. Mrs Ryland stalks these corridors checking us all in and out. Why do you have so many shoes? I just have a day and an evening pair for Phoebe and flat ones for me."

"There aren't that many," objected Jack. "Brogues for outdoor wear, plain and co-respondent for indoors. Leather pumps for dancing, tennis shoes, swimming shoes. It's hard to see how to do a week on the coast with much less. Where are you off to?"

"Next door. Phoebe requested early morning tea. I've left her until last so I can tidy her room while I drink it."

Jack chuckled. "How are you going to manage being in two places at once for the next few days?"

"Phoebe is the sort of modern young woman who never has breakfast. I imagine she toils away at her journalistic endeavours in her room all morning. Lucy, on the other hand, having done a full day's work by lunchtime, is going to develop a lousy headache and sleep for the rest of the day."

"And tomorrow?"

Lucy made an airy gesture indicating that tomorrow could take care of itself.

He grinned. "Did anyone spot you breaking into the staff block earlier?"

"Only Pyotr the gardener, mending his lawn after a group of bright young things danced on it all night. He rolled his eyes when he saw me and shook his head sadly. I did overhear something, though."

Jack listened to her account of the whispers in the stairwell with a frown. "I'll add it to the unexplained happenings list. If nothing else, it's an odd time of day to be having a discussion. Do you really have to go?"

She gave him an arch look. "My tea is getting cold. You know how I feel about cold tea. Incidentally, you won't have to avoid Veronique Carter over your eggs and bacon. I happen to know several of the top floor guests are breakfasting in their suites. The language in the kitchen is not complimentary. Oh, and there was a new huddle of staff at breakfast this morning. All Russian, to judge from the way they were listening intently to Grigory's instructions."

"Grigory?"

"Senior waiter and chief assistant to the maitre d'. Unofficial staff foreman on the Russian side. It was in the report I wrote for your uncle. Don't you ever read the letters I send you?" She blew him a kiss and left the room.

Jack drank his tea quickly, resigned to an hour's work on lists, notes and theories before he had to socialise. His uncle had instructed him to look for surprising circumstances. He and Lucy seemed to have amassed a respectable collection already. Before he began he strolled out on to his balcony, admired the trim gaff schooner swinging to anchor in the bay, shook his head over the madness of the early-morning fishermen already setting up on the jetty, and then gazed along at the other balconies. Lucy's intruder must have disappeared into one of these rooms, then out into the corridor without her seeing them. But why? What was special about her room. He looked back at her balcony, remembering vaulting over the dividing rail yesterday. He repeated the exercise and tapped on her window.

She reappeared, feather duster in hand. "Don't *do* that," she said. "I nearly spilled tea all down my apron."

"Sorry. I just wondered whether there were any middle-distance hurdle experts amongst the guests."

"You are more likely to know that than I am."

"Or amongst the staff?"

"I have no idea. Go back inside, Jack. I'm sure guests in pyjamas aren't supposed to flirt with chambermaids on hotel balconies."

"If you're worried the fishermen will see us, they won't. As soon as they cast they are mesmerised by the float and the water." Jack leaned against the corner rail and looked out. "See, blind to the rest of the world." He squinted at the flat top of the truncated Doric column in line with the railing. "Unlike me. The perfection of this hotel is bringing out my inner vandal. The temptation to balance a pot of scarlet geraniums on the ledge of that ridiculous ornamental boss, for instance, is immense. Is there a flower shop in town?"

"Yes, but Mr Delaney would have heart failure. Besides, it would blow off."

"What's it for, anyway?"

"The boss? Not being an architect, I wouldn't know. Do go, Jack. I really need to get on. Mrs Ryland's a tartar when she thinks we're slacking."

Jack took the hint and returned to his room.

Lucy emerged from room 19 shutting the door quietly behind her. "Miss Sugar doesn't want to be disturbed," she said to Irene.

Except it wasn't Irene who stood there, it was the head housekeeper. "Is everything satisfactory, Miss Brown? You were in there long enough."

Well, yes. It takes time to flirt with a passing playboy and polish off a tray of morning tea. "I was cleaning the bathroom, Mrs Ryland. The guest asked me to as she'd left it in a bit of a mess." Behind the housekeeper's back she saw Irene come out of a room at the far end of the corridor.

Irene looked horrified. Lucy wasn't surprised. Room 1 was one of Lucy's rooms and the housekeeper was very strict about her staff sticking to the rules, though the chambermaids gave each other a hand as a matter of course.

"Nobody is checking out on this floor today," said

Lucy, keeping Mrs Ryland's attention on her until Irene was clear of the door, "so we'll wait to clean the rest until the visitors are at breakfast."

The housekeeper gave a starched nod, turned and marched towards the stairs. "Your cap is crooked, Miss Trent," she said, "and your shoe has mud on the instep. See to it."

"Yes, Mrs Ryland," said Irene.

"What were you doing in there?" asked Lucy.

"He came out demanding fresh towels," said Irene in a low voice. "You were down the other end."

"Yes, Miss Sugar is going to work in room 19 this morning, so she asked me to do the bathroom straight away. What a cheek of room 1. He had fresh towels. I put them in there yesterday."

Irene rolled her eyes. "They were wet from his bath last night. He wanted dry ones. He has also changed his mind and wants tea. I'll take it in. He's testy enough without confusing him with extra chambermaids."

She rapidly assembled a tray from the trolley and disappeared down the corridor. Lucy thought cynically that either Irene was after a favour from her in return or the testy guest was a good tipper.

The morning wore on. As the guests went down for breakfast, Lucy and Irene serviced their rooms. Lucy was just backing out of room 3 with her basket of cleaning equipment when she heard the door to room 1 open.

"I've finished in here for now, but I'll be back in an hour," drawled the occupant.

Lucy's nerves jangled. "Very good, sir," she said, keeping her face averted. It was Xavier Hilliard, the man Jack had described as an upmarket moneylender, the man who had mesmerised Gina Bianca last night and deliberately targeted Veronique Carter to partner him in a dance. The man she herself had labelled as dangerous. He'd looked at her as Phoebe pretty sharply after she'd taken that photograph. She didn't want him seeing her as Lucy any too closely today. She reflected it was a good thing she'd been in her own room when he'd demanded a dry towel.

Mr Hilliard was evidently a man of tidy habits. His clothes were all hung up, his shoes lined neatly along the wall. She shook her head, marvelling at the vanity of men. He had even more footwear than Jack. The only disorderly note was struck by the bed, which looked very much like her own had this morning. Lucy raised her eyebrows at the absent Mr Hilliard. What a busy gentleman he must be. She somehow doubted it had been Miss Carter gracing his sheets. The heiress had *look, don't touch*, written all over her.

However, Lucy herself was in no position to pass judgement on how the guests spent their nights. She restored the bed to a pristine state, cleaned the bathroom and removed the tea tray, frowning as she put the used towels in the laundry hamper. Irene had been empty handed when she came out of this room earlier, and yet there had been no extra towels in the bathroom. Perhaps he'd thrown the wet one at her.

Lucy pushed aside her feeling of unease and went to give her friend a hand mopping up a shared bathroom that looked as though a water fight had taken place inside it.

Coming out, she spotted a fair-haired woman trying her own bedroom door. Heart banging, she sped along the corridor to stop her. "I beg your pardon, madam, but the guest in here said she didn't want to be disturbed this morning."

The woman spun around, dropping a key into her handbag. It was Gina Bianca. "Oh," she said blankly. "Am I on the wrong floor? I thought this was my room."

Oh really? "I'm afraid not, madam. Did you get out of the lift too soon, perhaps?"

"I must have done. How silly of me. Everything looks so alike." She darted a nervous glance down the corridor and hurried back around the corner to the lift.

Another odd thing to tell Jack. For an actress, Miss Bianca was a terrible liar. Not only was this nothing like the second floor, whose corridor was lit by windows overlooking the gardens, she'd had what appeared to be a staff pass key in her possession. Jack would be very interested in that. Lucy was more than a little interested herself. An intruder in here yesterday and Gina Bianca trying the door today. What was so special about her room?

CHAPTER FIVE

Jack watched Gina Bianca leave the dining room, puzzled. He prided himself on his ability to get along with anyone, which was why it was surprising that he'd made so little headway with her. He had dispensed the same effortless flow of trivia as always, but had received little more than monosyllables in return. It prompted him to study her a little closer. She wasn't as young as she appeared to be on screen, but she didn't seem jaded, she was simply unresponsive.

It was possible, of course, that the actress was not at her best at breakfast. This was understandable. It was also true that the Lester twins at the same table were chattering enough for a dozen people, but it was odd even so. He'd asked about her latest film, about what she was going to shoot next. He'd asked whether it was different making a film in America to making one in this country and was it true that they went around knocking on people's front doors when they wanted to film a crowd scene?

This last had drawn a response. "Oh, yes," said Gina, looking almost animated. "Some of the extras are shocking. They think they are the stars and push to the front and make faces."

"Maddening for you," Jack had said. "How do you manage?"

"Ronnie... that is, the production people keep them out of the way."

She'd stopped, flustered again, and buttered a piece of toast Jack was sure she didn't want. Who was Ronnie? The watchful type from yesterday? Then why wasn't he here, keeping an eye on his ewe lamb?

To Gina's evident relief, Amanda Lester had interrupted the non-conversation by asking whether Jack would like to take her and Julie on at tennis?

"Rather," said Jack. "When? Now? I'm going into town later to meet Charles off the train."

"That will be jolly. I adore Charles. Do you know Charles Bridgewater, Gina?"

"I don't think so. Will you excuse me? I'm not feeling very well." And so saying, she'd hurried away, leaving the toast untouched.

"Was it something I said?" Jack asked the twins.

"No," replied Julie. "She's being boring this week. I can't think why she came when she isn't enjoying herself."

"Perhaps she's pining for Jimmy," said Amanda. "Jimmy Ward, you must know him."

"Ward? Yes, I know him." *Amiable, sense of humour, possessed of a brain. And surprisingly on the list of residents.*

"He works with Daddy in the city. They're both coming up tomorrow morning. He's madly in love with Gina, but she's tied into some sort of contract with the film studio. Jimmy's frightfully maudlin about it."

"She seemed quite thick with someone else at tea yesterday," said Jack in a vague tone.

The twins exchanged glances. "That's her manager, I think," said Julie. "He's a bit... domineering. He's not staying here though."

"If he was, she wouldn't have been dancing with that smooth type last night," added Amanda. "Dreamy mover, wasn't he? Look, there he is, sitting with that awful Mrs Portman."

"Getting along very well with her too," commented Julie. "It ought to be a sin to look so sexy over breakfast, don't you think?"

"Indecent," agreed Amanda. "Which reminds me, Jack, why did you dance with Julie yesterday but not me?"

"I was about to ask you, naturally," said Jack, "but Hubert looked at me so menacingly I didn't dare."

Amanda whooped with laughter. "Hubert couldn't look menacingly at a cup of coffee. We'll meet you at the courts. See if you can beat up the tennis pro to make a four. Mummy said there was one on the staff."

Jack gave an ironic salute, asked about the pro at the desk and was told he could be found in the pavilion, then went upstairs to change into his tennis clothes. As he rounded the top banister, he saw Lucy staring in a perturbed fashion at the lift. Behind an open door came the sounds of a dustpan and brush being wielded. He raised his eyebrows in a query.

She darted a look at the open door. "Gina Bianca just tried to get into my room with a staff key," she muttered. "But it couldn't have been her yesterday because she was in the lounge with Mr No Photographs. I need to get on, sorry." She whisked around the corner with her basket of cleaning equipment.

Against all his instincts, Jack prevented himself from following her. His nerves rasped at how much he was hating this deception. That would need thinking about. For now he added the new information to the notes in his strongbox, changed into flannels and tennis shoes and headed for the pavilion, wondering how much more the Lester girls knew about Gina Bianca.

"Jack." Charles strolled along the platform, followed by a porter hauling a large trunk.

"Good God, how long are you staying?" asked Jack, eyeing this monstrosity.

"You neglected to tell me," replied his friend. "I thought I'd better be prepared."

"That's not going to fit on the charabanc. Send it to the Bay Sands Hotel," said Jack to the porter. "Room 17, if it will go through the door." And to his friend, "You and I are walking back."

"Have a heart. The railway coffee was terrible. I require immediate refreshment."

"Then we will call at the Resplendent. We may have to dodge Theo and Hubert, but at least we won't be overheard."

"Dear me, what have you been up to?"

"Not as much as I intend to be. How is your Russian? There is a rather interesting groundsman I'd like you to meet."

"Always happy to chat to any friends of yours. It's why I'm here. What makes him interesting?"

"I'm pretty sure he used to be an architect, back in the old country. It would be fascinating to learn how he wound up tending the lawn here. It'll take all your celebrated tact though. I had a couple of words with him this morning on my way to the tennis court. Not what I'd call a loquacious soul, though Lucy tells me he gave her a comprehensive lecture on the perils of a flat roof a couple of weeks ago."

"Can't blame him for that. Given the choice, I'd prefer to talk to Lucy than to you."

"You can talk to her later. For now you are stuck with me. If you don't get anywhere with Pyotr, the tennis pro is also of Russian extraction, as are the professional dancers and the majority of the waiters. It's quite an enclave and I'd like to know why. According to Lucy, they say it's nice to be with other Russians. She tells me another small group turned up this morning."

Charles looked thoughtful. "Now that is interesting. There has been a steady trickle of Russian types swelling the ranks in the east end of London over the last few months. They don't appear to be inciting unrest, but they are building in numbers. My superiors are getting a little restive about the point of entry, due to certain officious types in other branches levelling accusations of laziness and complacency at the port authorities."

"Uncle Bob is getting more than restive. He wants to know where they are coming from and with what intent. Lucy thinks the ones on the staff here are White Russians, not Bolsheviks, but it would be good to know for sure."

Charles shaded his eyes. "There appears to be a Victorian monstrosity looming up on us. I feel in my bones this must be the Resplendent."

"A deduction borne out by the large gold lettering across the facade. Is there no end to your talents? Let us see what they can do for us by way of sustenance. Charles, I hesitate to ask this, but can that possibly be the Earl of Elvedon having forty fits in the doorway?"

"Rupert? Yes, he was on the train," said Charles. "Two of his aunts are staying at the Bay Sands Hotel and have summoned him for a friendly chat about his Duty To The Family."

"Why has he obeyed?" said Jack. "Why hasn't he murmured meaningless promises and melted away in a whisper of expensive tailoring like he usually does?"

"He tells me his nerves are being utterly frayed by the constant onslaught from his relatives. Coming here to be jawed at is the lesser of several evils. These particular aunts can be relied on to deliver the family line in a civilised fashion over either tea or gin cocktails according to the time of day, then they will resume their bridge-play and he can be wafted back to London by tomorrow's train. The alternative was a phalanx of stronger-minded aunts descending on him at Elvedon Court and staying until a knot of superior distinction had been tied."

"There were signs of that at his father's funeral. We advised him to go abroad. Why hasn't he?"

"Because a dear, dear chum has written a splendid play that he wants Rupert to stage for him. They were hectically busy with it all last week, doing the rounds of the London theatres to find a sufficiently enlightened one. They didn't succeed. If the journey had been longer, no doubt I could furnish you with more details. As it was, I was profoundly glad Kingsthorpe station rounded the bend when it did."

Inside the Resplendent - surely named more in ambition than veracity by those early Victorians - they were accosted by Viscounts Nicholson and Jarmaine who proposed a spot of lunch before strolling up to the Bay Sands Hotel. So much for being able to talk to Charles in private.

"Truth to tell, we slept through breakfast," confessed Hubert. "Too much dancing on the lawn last night."

"Julie and Amanda," remarked Jack, "were not only up for a substantial breakfast, but have also played a set of tennis this morning."

"Then I definitely need lunch," said Theo. "Hello, there's Rupert. Couldn't you get in at the Bay Sands for this shindig either?"

Rupert tossed back his carefully tousled locks with a martyred air. "The Bay Sands Hotel is where my aunts are. If there is a shindig in the offing, I understand the location. They didn't tell me I would be staying in an offence to the eyes."

The launch wasn't the only thing in the offing, thought Jack. Wherever Mr Carter was, there was business going on behind the scenes, and right now he wanted a coronet for his daughter. Rupert's presence was unlikely to be a coincidence. He wondered what sort of inducement

Carter had made to the aunts to get them to Kingsthorpe. Certainly the chances of the realm's newest earl returning by tomorrow's train was negligible. "You'll like the Bay Sands," he assured him. "An art form made solid and turned into a hotel. If I were you I'd get the people here to call you a car and go up there straight away."

Rupert stared at him as if he'd run mad. "I hardly think so. These are my travelling clothes. I ought to be in a resort ensemble before I move another step. I'm feeling dreadfully uncomfortable already." He drifted away, shielding his eyes against the worst excesses of the heavy Victorian furniture.

"Lunch," said Charles. "If we hurry, we can eat and be on our way before he decides to join us. Two hours on the train in his company was quite enough exposure to the artistic muse for one day."

Lucy perched on the corner of Myrtle's desk, helpfully holding open the bookings register as Myrtle added early morning tea to Xavier Hilliard's account. "It makes a lot of work for you with a full hotel," she said, rapidly running her eyes over the names and room numbers and hoping she'd be able to remember them. "I saw at breakfast several more staff had arrived. That will help, I expect."

"They came last night," said Myrtle. "Two kitchen, two waiters, a maintenance man and two gardeners. None of them are office-based."

Lucy listened with half an ear. *Gina was in room 25. That was above room 1, so it was nonsense about her mistaking Phoebe's room for her own. It was Mr & Mrs Lester who had room 34 above Lucy.* "Oh, that's a shame. Can't you ask for an assistant?"

"I can manage mostly," said Myrtle. "We aren't always this busy, as you know."

"But you will be when the word goes around how nice it is here. Better to get ready now, I'd have thought."

"I suppose so. I'll ask Uncle Faun. Four of the new men have wives and some of them have children. I don't know how they are all going to fit in. Grigory says the families will stay in Mr Carter's boarding houses for now and refurbish them in lieu of rent. I suppose it's better than having children in the staff block, but I can't help worrying about them."

Myrtle spoke in a preoccupied tone, giving another little look through the glass window in the office door. She'd been doing so every time a shadow passed by, and every time she subsided with an air of disappointment.

The door opened. Lucy slid hastily off the desk as Mr Delaney came in and frowned to see her there.

"Room 1 had early tea, sir," she whispered, keeping her eyes lowered. "He hadn't ordered it, so I thought someone should know."

"Tea? Oh, very good. Myrtle, would you…?"

There was a booming shout from reception. Mr Delaney turned and hurried out. Through the open door, Lucy saw the large, fair-haired man of the night before hail him. Myrtle gave a infinitesimal whimper.

After a couple of words, Mr Delaney went quickly in the direction of the dining room and the fair-haired man came into the office.

"Good morning, Mr Karlsson," said Myrtle, looking very pink and pretty. There was nothing distracted about her now.

"Your uncle is organising more coffee for our meeting," he said, "so I am free to ask how is the most beautiful flower in England today?"

"You say the silliest things. I am very well, thank you. How are you and how is your mother? She wasn't very happy the last time you came over."

"She is cross because I have not yet brought her a nice biddable Swedish bride that she can find fault with and order to run her errands."

"I am sure she is not cross at all."

"I'd, er, better get back to work, Myrtle," murmured Lucy, but she was fairly confident her friend had forgotten she was there. However, the incursion of Mr Karlsson had been most useful. A swift perusal of the register and Lucy now knew the names of all the top floor visitors and which suites they were booked into. She also had the feeling Jack was going to be very interested to know about Mr Carter's boarding houses.

Delaney hurried into the dining room. The maitre d' said huffily that coffee had been delivered to the business meeting upstairs earlier and the waiter sent away with the instruction that they would serve themselves and send down again when they wanted more. It was not, he intimated with a portentous glare, what he had been used to.

Delaney spent several minutes sympathising, agreed that certain people had no idea of how to behave in a civilised fashion, but suggested that as these particular people were the ones who, in effect, paid all their wages, perhaps he could be very magnanimous and overlook it on this occasion.

As he spoke, a small part of his mind fretted about Myrtle chatting to that chambermaid. He'd seen the two of them together before. Give an impressionable girl some friends of her own age and her concentration would slip. Worse, she might start getting restless. Young women were so flighty nowadays. He didn't want Myrtle being influenced by any modern ideas. It was a pity none of the Russian women would take on chambermaid work, but

Grigory had been very definite. Good Russian girls, he had said, did not enter gentlemen's bedrooms when they were on foreign soil. Laundry, yes. Cleaning public rooms, yes. Nothing above the ground floor. One never knew, he had added darkly. One heard stories. It was well known that foreigners had lax morals.

Having extensive experience of the London hotel trade, Delaney had found himself unable to muster an argument to this, so as he needed Grigory to manage the Russian staff, English chambermaids it would have to be.

When he hurried back, Gustav Karlsson was still at the reception counter, looking idly through the hotel register while further down, young Quentin dealt with a gentleman who wished to hire fishing tackle and try his luck off the jetty.

"Good business this week," said the Swede.

"Very good," said Delaney. "The hotel is full. More coffee will be sent up. Will you all be lunching in the dining room?"

Karlsson looked at him with a merry twinkle in his eyes. "Aha! Rumbling in the kitchen, yes? I will ensure so. You will join me, perhaps? You and the little niece?"

"I will be delighted to. Myrtle, alas, has different luncheon arrangements."

Upstairs, Lucy was pondering the difficulty of telling Irene she had a dreadful headache and was going to lie down for the afternoon, whilst simultaneously changing into Phoebe up here and not walking over to the staff block with the other girls as usual. Another problem she had airily assumed would solve itself - until it didn't.

"Excuse me, miss," said a deep man's voice behind her. "You are the friend of Myrtle, I think?"

Lucy turned, startled, to see Gustav Karlsson addressing

her with a frowning air. Goodness, he was really very good-looking. He was also a regular visitor, in a top floor suite and friendly with Mr Delaney which pointed to him being a person of interest on several counts. "Yes, sir. That is I know her and talk to her sometimes when she is not too busy or when we are off duty. I like her awfully."

He gave a businesslike nod. "I too like Myrtle very much. I wish to speak with her alone, but her uncle is obstructive. I think if nothing is done he will keep her shut in that office until she fades away from lack of sun and good fresh air. I wish to court her, you understand. You say nothing to her, but persuade her out for lunch and I join you on the road, yes?"

Lucy gaped. This was the last thing she had expected. "Um, I suppose so. She doesn't have very long for lunch. We can just make it to the Seagull café and back in time. We've done that before."

That got a frown. "Talking while hurrying is not romantic. This is my heart I speak of. I wish Myrtle to be my wife."

"Oh." Lucy felt her own heart wobble at the simple sincerity on his face. "You could ask the kitchen for a picnic basket and take her to the dunes, perhaps? I will simply return to the hotel."

His face cleared. "You would do that? That is perfect. I will ask Grigory. Not today as I have a tedious meeting all afternoon. Talk, talk, talk while the waves are dancing and the sun shines and my boat calls me. That is businessmen for you. Tomorrow? One o'clock? Will she go with me?"

Lucy thought Myrtle would happily trot alongside Gustav Karlsson into the jaws of Jonah's whale if he asked her to. "I think so, yes."

"You are a good friend. My heart thanks you. Tomorrow at one o'clock." He nodded again and ran up the next flight of stairs.

He must really be in love, thought Lucy. There weren't many men who would arrange a romantic assignation in a busy hotel corridor with people passing to and fro. On the thought she bent to fiddle with her shoe as Mr Hilliard headed past, going towards his room. He, she thought, was a different type entirely. She wouldn't act as a go-between for him if he paid her.

She was suddenly visited by apprehension. Was she doing the right thing? Gustav Karlsson had seemed open and sincere, but what if it was an act? She *liked* Myrtle. She had been to Myrtle's home and had met Myrtle's mother, a faded woman who kept house for her brother and who liked Kingsthorpe much better than Kentish Town where Mr Delaney's previous hotel had been. He had always been ambitious, she'd confided with a sort of wondering pride. He'd been very good to her and Myrtle and Joe, after Alfred had met his end in the war. Her eyes had misted over at the memory. Training Myrtle up to the hotel business and getting young Joe an apprenticeship in the smart garage on the Skegness road. Much better prospects for him up here than back in Kentish Town. His old friends were now drudging in the cigarette factory where the hotel had used to be. Fauntleroy was happier too. No more money worries, not that he'd ever said, but you couldn't fool a sister who'd looked after you since you were three years old, could you? Myrtle had nodded and agreed that Uncle Faun had always been good to them.

Suppose Lucy was doing Myrtle a huge disservice? How could she be sure Mr Karlsson's intentions were honourable? Did white slave traders still exist? *"My boat calls me,"* he had said.

"What's up?" asked Irene. "Lost sixpence and found a farthing?"

"Headache," said Lucy, feeling a little sick. "I'm going to skip lunch and lie down for the afternoon, see if I can sleep it off. Luckily I've nearly finished here."

"You want me to save you something from the dining room?"

"No thanks. If it's what I think, I'm better off not eating."

Irene made a sympathetic face. "Well, at least it's me on towel duty later, so you can get a good rest. Hope you feel better tomorrow." She headed for the back stairs.

That was easier than she'd expected. Lucy made a mental note to ask Jack about Karlsson. Meanwhile, Phoebe was hungry.

CHAPTER SIX

Lucy ducked into the chambermaids' cubbyhole until the corridor was quiet, then let herself into Phoebe's room. Mrs Ryland had already been around for the day, so it would be quite safe to hide Lucy's uniform dress, apron and mob cap flat inside the bed.

She changed quickly, tied a pink chiffon scarf as a bandeau around the blonde wig and she was ready. Her sensible shoes she put at the back of the wardrobe behind Phoebe's evening shoes.

The dining room was well attended. Sadly, there was no chance of sitting within hearing distance of the table where Gustav Karlsson was lunching with Mr Delaney, the Carters and a gentleman who had the shrewd face of a businessman. Presumably the stylish lady with him was his wife, in which case they could be Mr & Mrs Mackenzie who had the roof-terrace suite overlooking the golf-course. As she watched, two more gentlemen were shown to the table. She would have taken long odds on them also having roof-terrace suites.

A waiter came up to her, apologised for there being no single places and wondered whether she might like to join the table of ladies by the window? Lucy acquiesced and found herself with a good view of the road and the company of four very smart women who were exhaustively discussing the morning's bridge hands.

They were joined a moment later by Gina Bianca and Mr No Photographs who were clearly in the middle of an argument. "I *told* you. I've been telling you for a fortnight," snapped Gina. "I have to and that's that. I don't have a choice."

Her companion glanced irritably at the occupants of the table. Lucy spread her hands as if to say *'Look, no camera'*. His mouth tightened, but he said nothing, pulling out his chair and throwing himself into it, leaving Gina to be seated tenderly and respectfully by the waiter. She smiled her thanks at him.

"And you're too free with your smiles," growled the man.

"I'm an actress. He might be a fan."

Which was, considered Lucy, a very restrained rejoinder. In Gina's place, she'd have thumped him. She gave her order to the waiter and looked around the room. The Lester girls were on an animated table by the door. Xavier Hilliard was also there, eating quickly and glancing at them with hooded amusement. Thalia Portman was having a lingering conversation with one of the waiters, directing the full force of her personality at him. For a moment Lucy toyed with the notion of making a voluptuous widow the victim in *Murder in the Palm Court Lounge* when she finally got around to writing it, but decided regretfully that it wouldn't do. It was already clear Mrs Portman wouldn't be anywhere except in her own expensive suite overnight. She was also - judging by comments from the top floor chambermaids - unlikely to be alone.

Lucy abandoned the idea and started to compose snappy sentences in her head for 'Society Snippets', beginning with a description of Mrs Mackenzie's very stylish outfit. Not for the first time, she wished she could lip read. She could see Gustav Karlsson talking energetically to his companions and had no idea what he might be saying. Such a waste. There was certainly more to him than met the eye. She just hoped for Myrtle's sake it was all on the level.

"Your soup," murmured the waiter.

"Thank you." Lucy returned her attention to her own table. Outside the wide windows, a cab drew up and a preposterously good-looking gentleman in a blazer and flannels alighted.

"Oh good," said one of the bridge-playing ladies without any evidence of enthusiasm. "Elvedon has arrived."

Her neighbour turned, made eye contact with the waiter and indicated that the newcomer should be shown to their table. "The sooner we get on with it, the sooner he'll take himself off," she remarked obliquely.

"Are you expecting another member of your party?" asked Lucy. "Would you like me to move up a place?"

"Do you mind? Thank you. So kind."

"This hotel is amazing," were the gentleman's first words on reaching the table. "It's an art form turned into reality. I wanted to transfer up here instantly, but they say there are no rooms free. Hello, Aunt Elvira. Salutations, Aunt Maude. Why didn't you tell me how splendid it is here?"

"I did," replied the woman nearest Lucy. "I said the Bay Sands Hotel was smart and modern and I thought it would amuse you. I also advised you to book early."

"Good afternoon, Elvedon" said the other aunt. "Did you have an agreeable journey?"

"Passable, thank you, Aunt Maude. There was a chap I knew on the train and I was telling him all about my friend Donnington's play." He stopped, the menu dropping from his hand. "That's it. This would be a topping place to stage it. Clear one end of that terrace affair outside and you've got the perfect backdrop." He looked around the table, focused on Gina Bianca and said, "Don't you agree, Miss Bianca? Performing outside to the accompaniment of the lapping waves. Fabulously avant-garde. What could be better?"

"Those lapping waves come with a sharp wind and occasional squalls of rain," drawled Mr No Photographs. "You had better build doctor's fees into your offer if you want Miss Bianca in the company."

Gina's eyes widened. "Are you crazy, Ronnie? Filming external scenes is bad enough, but a play goes on for hours. I'd freeze. And I'd have to remember lines!" She looked appalled at the very idea.

"I wasn't serious. No small-time outfit could afford you. And who wants to go to the theatre when there is a picture house in town with tickets at a quarter of the price?" He favoured the new arrival with a disparaging look. "The name's Oaks. I look after Miss Bianca's interests."

A name at last, thought Lucy, and not one she remembered seeing in the hotel register. Intriguing. It was also worth noting that whatever their private argument had been about, as soon as anything professional raised its head, Gina and Oaks were united.

The waiter returned with his order pad. The newcomer seemed prepared to interrogate him in depth about every item until one of the aunts said he would take the soup, followed by the cutlets.

"It is no use prevaricating, Elvedon," she said. "By the time you made up your mind supper would be being served and we should all have starved to death."

Elvedon. Lucy's interest was piqued. Not the new Earl of Elvedon, by any chance? That was a stroke of luck. A paragraph about him for 'Society Snippets' would be very well received by her editor. He'd only succeeded to the title a few months ago when his father, a man in the prime of life, had succumbed to measles of all undignified things, followed closely by his older brother. Before that, Rupert Manners had only been of peripheral interest to the readers of the *Chronicle*, being an artistic dilettante rather than a society catch. Eying his clothes and listening to his stage-strewn conversation, Lucy didn't think much had changed.

The earl could certainly talk. Lucy had finished her lunch and was waving away the dessert options by the time Lord Elvedon's Aunt Elvira pointed out that his soup was growing cold.

He looked at it in surprise. "I must have been in one of my enthusiasms," he remarked.

"That's one word for it," said Mr Oaks dryly.

"With the estate to look after, you should be concentrating on the land, not the stage," said Aunt Maude. "It is your duty to the family to keep it in order."

"But the theatre is my life," declaimed Lord Elvedon. "What are estates compared to art?"

Lucy jumped as a hand clasped her shoulder. "Do excuse me for interrupting," said a cut-glass voice, "but I noticed you had finished your meal, Miss Sugar, and I wondered if you were leaving a vacant place? I couldn't help overhearing the theatre mentioned. It is a passion of mine. Such a shame there isn't one in Kingsthorpe."

Lucy stood, amused by Veronique Carter's sheer effrontery. "It is, isn't it? Do please take my seat. I'm off for a stroll in the grounds."

"Thank you." Miss Carter summarily dismissed her and awarded the earl a full blast of charm. "Don't you agree with me, Lord Elvedon?"

Across the dining room, Mr Carter, Mr Karlsson and the other gentlemen at their table were getting to their feet in the manner of men about to have a business meeting. Mr

Carter called Grigory over, tapped his watch and pointed in an upwards direction. Grigory nodded. Lucy remembered the regret in Gustav Karlsson's eyes when he mentioned *talk talk talk*. That would be why Veronique was here then. She was looking for someone to keep her amused for the afternoon. The Earl of Elvedon was undoubtedly easy on the eye and had been addressing Gina almost exclusively. Lucy wouldn't dream of suggesting that the heiress to a tobacco fortune was spoilt, but she rather thought there was some jealousy on Veronique's part here.

She left the dining room, wondering if Jack had returned. In the reception hall, Thalia Portman, now magnificently wrapped in furs, was ordering a private car to take her for a motor around the countryside.

"With a hamper in reserve in case we don't make it back for tea. Just champagne and a few sandwiches. And a thick rug," she said. Her eyes devoured young Quentin behind the desk.

Lucy, who had heard eye-popping accounts from the other chambermaids at breakfast about Mrs Portman's previous stay at the Bay Sands Hotel, was assailed by an image which she was pretty sure Quentin shared, judging by the way he was easing his collar. A voice behind her caused her to turn.

"Miss Sugar, I was wanting a little word with you. Will you join me in the lounge for coffee?"

Lucy was astonished. "Thank you, Mrs Lester. I should be delighted." Now this really was intriguing. What on earth did a woman securely at the heart of society want of a gossip columnist? There was only one way to find out.

"So, that's the story so far," said Jack as they strolled along the coast road. Theo and Hubert had gone on ahead and Rupert, thankfully, hadn't been seen since he'd wafted upstairs at the Resplendent in search of his luggage. "I don't know I'm any the wiser, but if the Bay Sands Hotel isn't a cover for something I'll give up investigative reporting and take up professional bridge."

Charles looked amused. "It's what people think you do anyway. I'll see if I can get a line on these Russians, but I'm not hopeful. They tend to be close-mouthed and clannish unless one has a way in."

"Meanwhile, we infiltrate the edges of the inner circle and keep our ears open. I'd like to scout around the top floor, but Lucy says Edward Carter's secretaries are up there all the hours they aren't asleep."

"Pity. Is this it?" Charles stopped as they rounded the bend into the bay.

"The one and only Bay Sands Hotel. What do you think?"

"Very modern, very sleek, suits the coastline."

"Surprisingly so."

"It's out of place for all that." Charles moved forward again. "Nice gaff cutter moored in the bay. That won't have been cheap. Does it belong to the hotel?"

"I don't think so. It wasn't there yesterday, but it was this morning. It's possible Delaney organises excursions along the coast by sea as well as by road. Let us saunter towards the jetty in order to irritate those optimistic fishermen and admire it some more."

"Any particular reason?" said Charles, dropping his voice as they passed a well-dressed couple alighting from a car. A porter hurried out to deal with their luggage.

"It occurs to me that from the far end of the jetty one could get a tolerable view of the terraces belonging to the rooftop suites."

"Only if one has a pair of naval-issue binoculars about one's person," said Charles.

"We shall have to make do with the naked eye."

"Or you could allow me to unpack."

Jack looked at him with amusement. "You brought some?"

"Possible nefarious business on the coast, you said. Naturally I brought binoculars. The logical conclusion is some form of sea-going vessel will be involved. Apropos of which, the closer we get, the more I would like a look at that cutter on my own account."

"Idle interest?"

"It's not a British design. Aha," Charles paused on the jetty with satisfaction. "Do you see what this bijou launch says? *Tender to Krista.* I thought as much. *Krista,* if I am not mistaken..."

"Which you rarely are," murmured Jack.

Charles inclined his head, acknowledging the truth of this statement. "*Krista* belongs to a perfectly above-board Swedish merchant ship owner by the name of Karlsson. He often acts as his own master and makes regular runs to Immingham in his cargo steamer, all such runs being fully accountable. The difference between him and other similarly occupied masters is that instead of seeing to the whole process himself, he keeps *Krista* in Immingham and takes off in her for two or three days, while his Swedish cargo is unloaded and then the new cargo loaded under the supervision of his first mate. Do you know him?"

Jack smiled. This was more like it. "Not personally, but I have it on good authority that he's based in Lysekil, Sweden, and looks like Douglas Fairbanks Jr."

"Staying here, perchance?"

"On the top floor. He's a regular visitor but not, interestingly, a member of the consortium." Jack turned and gazed blandly at the hotel. "I wish you hadn't packed the binoculars. Couldn't you have bird-watched out of the train windows all the way up?"

"No," replied Charles. "Why?"

"Because I rather think a gentleman in a white pullover and bags is crouched in a furtive fashion between the two windows of the forward-facing roof-terrace suite. He appears to be stretching upwards, then hunching down and writing something. Both windows are open and one, according to Lucy, is Carter's office."

Charles continued to stare out to sea. "Can you make out who it is?"

"Not a hope. He's very well camouflaged. If he hadn't moved, I might not have spotted him. I wonder if I can accidentally ask the lift attendant for the wrong floor and get myself borne up there."

"I don't see how that will help. You can hardly stroll through someone else's suite to the terrace, checking on potential eavesdroppers."

"You're right. I'll find Lucy instead and see if she has learnt anything new."

"And I," said Charles, "shall ramble around the grounds brushing up my Russian."

"How did your afternoon go?"

"Very strangely," said Lucy. She and Jack were in her room swapping notes on what they had discovered since this morning.

"In what way?" asked Jack.

"Mrs Lester buttonholed me straight after lunch and kept me pinned in the lounge for a good two hours. I'm still reeling from it."

"What did she want?"

"The substance was The Wedding. She doesn't want the twins or the guests to be mobbed by the press. Supposing, she asked, that the *Chronicle* were offered exclusive photos. Would they be in a position to fend the other rags off?"

Jack looked at her with a lively interest. "Mrs Lester

wants to hire a gossip columnist to act as a gamekeeper? I don't believe it."

"Not precisely. Amidst the delicate hints and allusions, I gathered the passing of filthy lucre is intended to be in the other direction."

"Good lord. How very enterprising of her. I suppose keeping two debs up to the mark is expensive, but Lester makes enough for both of them, I would have thought."

"The rate those girls go through clothes, one can always use a little more. She's a bit scary, to be honest. She's the sort of woman my mother would have liked to be, dedicating her life to getting her daughters married into the aristocracy. What is she going to do after the wedding, with no more reason to dress them well and be seen in all the right places? She'll be lost. I must tell my mama I did her a favour by embracing independence all those years ago. I wouldn't conform, so she was forced to concentrate on my older brothers and their children instead of on me. As a result, she makes a splendid grandmother. I'm not sure Mrs Lester will do as good a job."

"What did you say to her?"

"To Mrs Lester? What could I say? That I would contact the *Chronicle*, of course. But Jack, that could all have been done inside half an hour. As it was, she pussyfooted around the subject for more like two hours and I had the feeling that not only was she hating every minute, but none of it was what she actually wanted at all. Do you think that counts as an odd circumstance?"

"If *you* think so, then yes it is. I'll add it to the list."

"She only stopped when Julie and Amanda came in gasping for tea because they'd been practising a new dance routine and were parched. Lots of other guests came into the lounge around then, so I was glad to escape in case any of them recognised me."

Jack frowned. "I thought you said no one would."

"They wouldn't recognise me as normal-Lucy, but Mr Hilliard was amongst them and he has got very shrewd eyes. I don't trust him. Gina was there too. I spoke to her as chambermaid-Lucy this morning, as well as lunching at her table as Phoebe. It's getting just a bit complicated."

"And likely to be more so. Charles and I saw someone lurking on the roof terrace when we arrived, crouched down by Carter's open window. I might suggest to Veronique that she holds a select cocktail party up there so I can see the lay of the land. I was going to wangle you an invitation too, but…"

"Please don't. You may not have any luck with a cocktail party. I think there are business meetings going on up there. Oh, you'll like this. Miss Carter was at a loose end after lunch and developed a spontaneous interest in the theatre so she could cut Gina out with Lord Elvedon. Not that Gina was particularly enthralled by him, but the earl was talking to her which Miss Carter was not impressed with at all. A touch of the green-eyed monster, I thought."

"She does like her coterie of followers. Charles was stuck with Rupert on the train. He said he was heading up here."

"He joined two of the bridge-playing ladies on my table. Aunt Maude and Aunt Elvira. I got the impression it was a duty lunch on their part. They perked up tremendously when Veronique muscled in."

"I'm not surprised. From what Charles said, these aunts have been deputised to remind Rupert of his duty. The family is very keen on him settling down and producing an heir, which may be a non-starter given his inclinations." He looked thoughtful. "Edward Carter wants a title for his daughter. I wondered if there was some manipulation to get Rupert here."

"How could there be?"

"Carter moves in mysterious ways. I can see him

offering Rupert's aunts a special deal on hotel rates in order to synchronise their visit. How do you know he is having a business meeting?"

Lucy told him about Gustav Karlsson and her deductions. "And now I'm worried whether I'm doing the right thing by Myrtle," she fretted.

"He would hardly have involved you if he wasn't on the level. Charles says Karlsson is a legitimate merchant seaman. I could bear to know his connection with the Bay Sands Hotel. Meanwhile, who in this place has a white pullover?"

"No idea. I can check my rooms when I clean tomorrow morning. Are you sure your eavesdropper wasn't wearing a white shirt? Everyone has one of those."

Jack looked gloomy. "It could have been. Hey ho, I shall go and drink tea and sweet-talk Veronique. See you at dinner."

Left to herself, Lucy lifted the telephone receiver and entered into a discussion with the switchboard operator about the possibility of putting through a call to the London office of the *Chronicle*. A scoop was still a scoop, no matter what the reason for it being presented to you on a plate.

CHAPTER SEVEN

For a hotel that still had two full days to go until its grand opening ball, the Bay Sands was dazzling with colour, jewels, cocktails and chatter.

"Phoebe Sugar is hardly going to need her flashbulb this evening," commented Jack to Charles as they entered the bar.

Charles nodded. "I haven't seen so many sparklers on show since the last ambassadorial reception at the palace."

"All trying to outshine each other. Hello, we've been spotted. The fair Veronique is smiling graciously at us. I think we take that as an invitation."

"Most definitely. Did you wangle a free pass to the top floor?"

"I broached the idea of holding one of her amusing cocktail parties on the roof, but she was too busy quizzing Rupert on his designs for a theatre to give it her full attention. She made vague maybe-tomorrow noises and continued to discuss the difference between a private theatre at one's home and a commercial venture. At a seaside resort town, for instance. Possibly at the end of a smart new pier."

Charles looked startled. "She's crazy. It would cost a fortune."

"I don't think that is an issue where a coronet is at stake." He raised his voice. "Miss Carter, as dazzling as ever." He inclined his head over her hand.

"Mr Sinclair. You and Mr Bridgewater are both invited to drinks tomorrow in my suite. Father thought it was a splendid idea. The setting couldn't be better."

Jack made gratified noises. "I shall look forward to it."

"Evening, Rupert," said Charles. "Still here, I see."

"I've been back to change, naturally. It's very inconvenient. The Resplendent hasn't got anything like the artistic ambience of this hotel. I felt my inspiration draining away by the minute as I was bathing and dressing. I daresay by tomorrow morning it will have withered and died completely, smothered by heavy damask curtains and gothic wardrobes."

"Too tragic," said Veronique. "I'll have a word with Father and see what he can arrange."

Jack refrained from quipping that if anyone was equal to redecorating Rupert's room at the Resplendent by midnight, it was Edward Carter. He glanced around the room, wondering where Lucy was.

"Good evening, Miss Carter, may I say how elegant you look. I hope I may have the pleasure of dancing with you again tonight."

As the smooth tones of Xavier Hilliard entered the conversation, Jack intensified his expression of affable blankness.

"Certainly," said Veronique. "You dance very well."

Was it Jack's imagination or did Hilliard's nostrils flare very slightly at the implication that he was good enough to dance with, but not necessarily to converse or dine with.

"I am enchanted that you think so," said Hilliard, "but with such a partner, it is hardly an effort."

Veronique preened, accepting the compliment as her due, and turned back to Rupert.

Hilliard's eyes flickered. Jack's gaze followed him as he drifted off. Presently he saw him infiltrate the group around Mr Carter and lean close to murmur in his ear. The effect was extraordinary. Edward Carter looked up sharply, said something to his companions and moved aside with Hilliard. He had the most inscrutable face of anyone Jack had ever met. There was nothing to indicate whether Xavier was broaching a business deal worth hundreds of pounds or discussing the merits of golf versus whist as a gentleman's pastime.

Whatever it was, the conversation seemed to have afforded Hilliard a certain amount of pleasure. There was a hooded satisfaction to him as he sauntered away. Carter was less easy to read. He kept his eyes on the dapper, elegant back, then signalled to one of his secretaries who was enjoying a blameless glass of beer in a corner of the bar. The young man hurried over, listened, looked dismayed, but left the room obediently. By shifting position, Jack could see him speaking to Fauntleroy Delaney across the reception counter before heading for the stairs.

More and more interesting, thought Jack as within a few minutes the hotel manager worked his way adroitly around the customers in the bar, stopped for a word with Mr Mackenzie and moved on. Mackenzie cast a single glance at Carter, then continued his conversation with Mr Forrest.

Jack nursed his drink, making it last in order to keep his wits about him, but nothing else out of the way occurred. It was significant, however, to find in the dining room that Mr Carter was not eating with the gentlemen of the consortium, but instead joined his daughter and a selection of her friends. Amongst this number, unsurprisingly, was Lord Elvedon. What *was* intriguing was the inclusion of Xavier Hilliard. Jack found it impossible not to connect this circumstance with the conversation between Hilliard and Carter in the bar.

On the strength of having played bridge with Mackenzie and Forrest in various London clubs, he took a spare chair at their table. Charles, as they had agreed, headed for Gustav Karlsson. The introduction of sailing and shipping into the dinner conversation might bore their companions, but it should establish amicable relations between the two.

It was a variation of the manoeuvres he and Charles regularly carried out when gathering information, but at the back of his mind this time was a fret of worry. Where was Lucy? What had happened? She should have been down by now.

Lucy, at that precise moment, was sitting in one of the deep reception chairs, making notes of all the things she had discovered in the last half hour, including a rather interesting conversation that had taken place at the reception counter itself.

The evening had started innocuously enough. She had bathed, dusted herself lightly with Phoebe's talcum powder, dressed and emerged from her room ready to go downstairs when she'd heard the discreet ring of the bell in the chambermaids' cubbyhole. The habit of the last three weeks had her automatically turning towards it. She realised her mistake and was able to spin around a split second before Irene came out to answer the summons.

"You have got to quit this job," she muttered to herself just as Xavier Hilliard's voice stopped her in her tracks.

"In here. I've got a job for you."

He was addressing Irene. Lucy breathed again, wondering what he wanted and why his tone was so peremptory. Whatever it was, she hoped he tipped her friend well. She hesitated. Jack was interested in Mr Hilliard... and they hadn't quite shut the door. Dare she listen? She sprinted down the corridor.

To her astonishment she heard Irene hiss, "I can't do it until the end of my shift. If Mrs Ryland rings through and I'm not here, I'll get the sack with no references."

"How pathetic of you. Your trouble is you don't think big enough."

"You try thinking big when you've got a kid and a sick mother to support," returned Irene. "That's why I'm in this mess."

Lucy was rocked to her core. That was not the tone of a chambermaid who had only met a guest for the first time this morning. Which meant they already knew each other. How? What was going on?

Hilliard laughed. "Lucky for me, wasn't it? Get on to it."

That sounded like an order and the close of a conversation. Lucy looked at the long corridor and frantically whisked into the side stairwell, forgetting until she heard a snatch of Russian conversation below her that only the staff used these stairs as a rule.

"All is new. There is little to do," said one of the Russians.

Maintenance men, probably. Even so, she couldn't risk passing any of her fellow workers face to face. She'd have to go upwards, along the second floor and down by the main staircase.

Or would she? Should she not wait until Irene's stint on towels finished and then follow her? It wouldn't be easy, though, and she was going to feel really stupid if Hilliard had merely asked her friend to take his shirts to the laundry. As she stood irresolute, the men below started climbing. Second floor it was, then.

As always, the late sunshine slanting through the corridor windows caught her by surprise. She snorted, thinking of Gina Bianca this morning saying the floors all looked alike.

There was an echoing snort on the other side of the first bedroom door.

It came again. It wasn't a snort, it was a sob. Someone in that room was crying, quietly and desolately. The number on the door was 25. That made it Miss Bianca's room. She sounded heartbroken. It went against the grain for Lucy not to tap on the door and try offering some comfort, but she didn't quite see how she could. No film star was going to want a gossip columnist knowing she was unhappy, still less tell her the reason why. Troubled, Lucy continued towards the main stairs. Perhaps Jack might be able to charm the actress into a happier frame of mind. She'd have a word with him later.

She caught a glimpse of washed-out blue as she walked quickly past the chambermaid's cubby. Like Irene downstairs, whoever was on duty up here would be bound to recognise her. However, guests were coming out of bedrooms now, dressed for an evening of amusement, so she could mingle and be lost in the crowd.

"Hello, Phoebe. I didn't know you were on this floor."

Julie Lester. Wonderful. "I'm not," said Lucy. "I'm exploring. Your corridor is prettier than mine."

"Have you seen upstairs?" said Amanda, joining them. "Seriously luxe. We wanted Mummy to book us a suite, but she said they were all taken and anyway, we aren't made of money."

"Which is odd, when you think about it, because that's what Daddy does, make money."

"Come and look at it now. Someone might have left their door open."

"And they might not. You are a goose, Amanda. Do let's go down, the boys will have arrived."

"It's a shame they couldn't get into the hotel here," said Lucy.

"We only just managed it ourselves. Mummy didn't

decide to come until the last minute. We were ever so surprised, because she'd said she didn't think it was smart enough to be worth bothering, but then she came back from town one afternoon saying to pack for the coast."

"And then it was put off, then it was on again. Coo-ee, Hubert! Have you missed me?"

"Desperately," said Viscount Jarmaine, standing up from where he and Theo had been waiting for their fiancées in the reception hall. "Listen, this is important. If Rupert suggests we sit with him at dinner, make an excuse. Some fool has been puffing him up with ideas about opening a theatre here. He refused to talk about anything else all the way to the Resplendent and all the way back again. I'm not saying a new pier wouldn't be jolly, but if I have to listen to any more of his theatrical piffle, I'll string him up with one of his own pulleys."

"So masterful," murmured Amanda admiringly.

"You can mock," said Theo. "You haven't heard him. Never been so nauseated in my life."

Julie patted his hand. "Poor babies. What you both need is a nice drink."

"Now you're talking," said Theo, brightening up, and the four of them went into the bar.

Lucy hung back. Xavier Hilliard had evidently finished with Irene and had come downstairs while she was taking the long route around. He was standing just inside the doorway and she had no desire to get too close to him. Veronique Carter's light laugh sounded above the murmur of conversation. Hilliard's head turned in that direction much as the stallions on her brother's stud scented the air when they caught a trace of a promising mare.

Outside the glass entrance of the lobby, Mr Oaks was staring upwards at the hotel balconies. Lucy wondered again why he wasn't staying here and whether it had been him who had made Gina Bianca cry. She also wondered if she could manage to get an accidental shot of him by taking a photograph of the impressive frontage of the Bay Sands itself. It was worth a try. She could certainly get a passing snap as she paused behind a concealing stand of palm fronds.

The tide had come in. As she walked out into the still air, Lucy heard the water make quiet rippling rushes up the beach. How nice it would be just to sit on the warm sand in the evening sunshine with Jack, brushing hands now and again and talking about everything and nothing. Would he like that too? The thought brought her up short. She had no idea. She had known him three months - how could she not be aware of such a basic facet of his character? It brought it home to her how little time they had actually spent together. In a sudden state of perturbation she turned and focused her camera on the Bay Sands Hotel.

A grating voice at her side said, "I thought I said no photographs."

Lucy jumped, furious that she'd nearly dropped her precious camera, furious that she'd been so exercised in her mind over Jack and his feelings for her that she hadn't noticed Mr Oaks abandon his scrutiny of the hotel and move across to her. "I'm getting a shot of the Bay Sands for my article," she snapped. "The sooner I do it, the sooner I can go indoors to eat."

He took a cigarette from his case and lit it. "Go on then. Earn your caviare and oysters."

Lucy felt her temper rise. If he was treating her as a hired hand, she would do the same for him. "I will if you move out of the way. I don't like people breathing down my neck while I work. I also don't like the idea of you blowing smoke across the camera lens at the critical moment. Films cost money. I don't get reimbursed for wasted photographs."

Oaks stepped back. "Quite the fighter, aren't you?"

"I'm a professional. Let me get on with my job."

"Got any pictures of Miss Bianca on that thing? Was she with anyone?"

"No," said Lucy in a bored tone. "I was going to ask her tonight how she wanted to pose."

He gave an unpleasant laugh. "Yeah, she'll be sure not to do herself a disservice there. I want to see it before it is used."

Did he think she carried a portable darkroom about with her? "That's not up to me, it's up to the *Chronicle*. Leave me alone, there's a good chap. I'm simply doing what I'm paid for."

Oaks muttered an oath about the uselessness of all women, and her in particular, drew on his cigarette and turned on his heel towards the town.

Lucy kept her back to him, listening to the receding sound of his brogues on the path. She was surprised to find she was shaking.

Inside the reception hall again, she sat in one of the deep chairs to put her camera back in its padded carrier and regain her composure.

One of Mr Carter's secretaries hurried out of the bar and leant over the reception desk. "Delaney," he called. "I'm taking dinner upstairs and I have a message for you from Mr Carter."

"Certainly, Mr Benton. I will inform the dining room. What is the message?"

"Mr Carter asks that you go into the bar and let Mr Mackenzie know quietly that he will not be dining with them. Tell him things are known which should not be, so Mr Carter is taking precautionary measures."

"Immediately, Mr Benton."

Lucy kept her head bent over her notebook, but by dint of looking sideways under lowered lashes, she saw the secretary hurry up the stairs and Mr Delaney come out from behind his counter and glide into the bar.

A car drew up outside, disgorging an extremely noisy party. That was useful. She could finish writing her notes - including Mr Carter's message - while they divested themselves of wraps and overcoats, then slip into the dining room, using them as cover.

From his place next to Mrs Mackenzie, Jack watched one of the waiters show Lucy to a table near the door. It would be nice, he thought with irritation, to be able to sit next to her openly for once, to laugh with her and joke, to listen to how her latest murder mystery was taking shape. To be normal.

Instead he smiled sympathetically at his neighbour's perorations on the Kingsthorpe shops and said he'd taken a walk through the town with his friend earlier and noticed indications that quite a few of the outlets were sharpening themselves up.

"That's Mr Mackenzie's doing," she said with a nod of her head. "I said to him when we first came to look at the area that you can always tempt people to the coast with promises of good food and gambling, but if you want to keep them here, you have to give them something to do during daylight hours as well as at night. Kingsthorpe might have been all the rage when Edward Carter stayed here as a child, but these days the place needs a good shake up to stop folk taking the next train back to town. When I put it like that, Mr Mackenzie saw my point and started making enquiries of the local agents. They've been pleasantly surprised at the possibilities." She shook her head tolerantly. "My husband and his friends work very hard, Mr Sinclair. They don't always understand that other people have time to fill."

Shopping being the smart set's recreation of choice, presumably, when they weren't playing bridge or golf or reading magazines on the terrace. Jack wondered just how many shops and other properties the consortium had bought up. What were they planning to do with them all? "He is a lucky man to have such a perspicacious wife," he replied.

"He always acknowledges it, that I will say. One of the new shops is a jeweller. They have a top craftsman to run it and Mr Mackenzie gave me this pretty thing to thank me for the idea." She extended her wrist to show Jack a fine bangle of linked sapphires and diamonds.

"A generous present indeed," said Jack admiringly. "Beautiful stones."

At the table behind them, Edward Carter's voice sounded in a lull in the conversation. "They tell me the weather is due to be fine tomorrow. Why don't you organise one of your tennis tournaments, my dear? There seem to be enough decent players here to make it a success. I can spare you Kirk and Benton if you need them."

"They would be useful and there is nothing I would like more," said Veronique, "but it's our cocktail party in the evening, don't forget."

"I don't see a problem with that. You are holding it in your sitting room, are you not? If you are engaged with the tennis tournament during the afternoon, it will give Grigory a free hand to set everything up without his team getting in your way. By the time you come back to change, it will be a done thing."

Veronique gave her tinkling laugh. "How clever you are, Father. Yes, that will be perfect. Do you play tennis, Rupert? I am sure you must do."

Jack masked a grin. They had progressed to first name terms, had they? That would please her father.

"Certainly. I shall have to remember to bring my tennis

gear with me in the morning. Such a bore, this going to and fro."

"Oh yes, I was going to ask you, Father. Can't anything be done about finding Rupert a room at the Bay Sands Hotel?"

"I'll see what I can manage, my dear. Do you play tennis, Mr Hilliard?"

"Very indifferently, I'm afraid, but naturally I shall be delighted to support the tournament if that would be useful to Miss Carter."

"Tennis," said Mrs Mackenzie with a faint sigh. "Ah well, I daresay it will be amusing to watch."

CHAPTER EIGHT

Lucy stood inside the doorway of the Palm Court lounge after dinner, ostensibly readying her camera. She was thus perfectly placed to catch Jack's eye as he strolled in from the dining room.

"I have news," she breathed. "Also a favour to ask. Gina Bianca is unhappy. Can you dance with her and find out why? Or at least cheer her up."

"Unlikely," murmured Jack. "She gave my best line of patter the complete cold shoulder this morning. Try Charles. Or have a go yourself. See you upstairs later to compare notes."

Lucy lifted her camera as if she hadn't heard him and moved in the direction of the band. Gina was sitting half-way down the room. She had repaired her face with professional skill, but behind the lovely mask her eyes were wary.

"Miss Bianca," said Lucy in a warm voice. "I'm supposed to be taking photographs of notable guests for the *Chronicle,* and I realised I haven't got one of you yet. You are such a favourite with 'Society Snippets' readers, they'll never forgive me if I miss you out. May I take your photograph, please? Where would you like to be?"

"Somewhere else," muttered Gina, then came to with a start. "Sorry. Let me see..."

Lucy's heart was wrung. She sat down in a chair next to her and smiled for the benefit of any observers. "Can I help?" she asked softly. "I'll go away if you like, but you don't look happy and really I'm very discreet. I wouldn't get far in my job by betraying the very socialites I'm paid to take nice pictures of."

"Sweet of you, but nobody can help. Yes, a photograph is always good publicity. Where do you suggest?"

"Listening to the band? Or maybe dancing?" She paused and drew a bow at a venture. "I happen to know Mr Oaks has gone back into Kingsthorpe for the evening."

Gina looked startled. "How did you...? Oh, you were at lunch. You heard us arguing. Ronnie is so difficult. He doesn't see being agreeable to people is part of my job. He wasn't supposed to be here this week. I told him not to come. How can I relax between films when he's watching me all the time?" She looked despairingly around the lounge. "About the only person I'd be safe to be pictured dancing with as far as he is concerned is the Earl of Elvedon. Ronnie says he's..." She broke off in confusion.

"So I'm told," replied Lucy. "That's another thing I would never refer to in my column. I wouldn't try it though, not unless you want to make an enemy of Miss Carter. How about Mr Bridgewater? He's frightfully photogenic and is seen simply everywhere."

She was amused to see Gina size up Charles shrewdly. "He would be good. Nice features. Wears his clothes well. Do you know him? Would he play along?"

Lucy smiled and stood up, extending her hand to the other girl. "I find brazen effrontery and the element of surprise goes a long way in my profession."

Gina gave an unforced laugh. "Always. It's how I got my first job in the pictures. Before that I was on the stage. *'Front row of the chorus, dear, lots of leg but for the love of us all, don't sing.'* You're all right, aren't you? Is it your real name?"

"Absolutely not. My parents would be horrified if they knew what I did for a living. They think I'm a typist."

"I thought it couldn't be. It takes one to know one. I'm Jean, really. The film company thought Gina sounded better. And Bianca instead of White." She paused. "You're lucky, having parents who'd mind. I lost Ma when I was twelve. Pa drank himself to death a couple of years later. One of the grannies down our street said I should train as a dancer. She'd been one. She knew an agency. It wasn't really dancing and I had to lie about my age but it was the stage and... well, you have to do what you can to survive, don't you?" Gina caught her breath. "And if you're not careful, it comes back to bite you. It's why I like acting. For a while I can be someone else."

"You're very good at it. Mr Bridgewater, good evening. I'm Phoebe Sugar. We met on the Atlantic Princess. Do you think you could help us? I'm supposed to be taking a society shot of Miss Bianca and we wondered if you could possibly pose with her as if you were about to whisk her into a foxtrot?"

Whether Jack had briefed him or not, Charles behaved beautifully. "My dear Miss Sugar, you are the answer to a film goer's prayer. I have been puzzling all day how I might introduce myself without offence. Miss Bianca, I believe I have seen all your pictures and would be delighted to help you out. If I may go further, once the photograph has been executed, I should be equally delighted to twirl you about the room for real."

It would have been impossible for even a hardened battleaxe to withstand Charles at his most charming. Gina was no battleaxe. She relaxed, gave Charles her hand, stood where Lucy directed with the suggestion of the band to one side of them and assumed a vivacious stance.

"Splendid," said Lucy. She took two shots and left them to continue the dance while she slipped away. She'd been quite visible enough for one day.

She hadn't been long in her room when there was a tap at the door. It was Jack.

He looked at her ruefully. "You're in Lucy clothes. Does that mean Phoebe is fading out for the night?"

Lucy nodded. "I'd quite like her to fade out completely," she confessed. "These are your friends, Jack."

He sat in the chair and met her eyes. "I know. I've thought of that too. We'll work something out. Meanwhile, what have you got?"

Lucy told him, and gave him the pages of her notebook to put in his safe.

"You're sure about the message from Edward Carter? 'Things are known which should not be'."

"That's what the secretary said, with the instruction to pass it on to Mr Mackenzie."

Jack put the notes away slowly. "Taken together with what I witnessed, it looks very much as if Xavier Hilliard has found out something about the consortium that they would rather have kept to themselves. I wonder what?"

"If nothing else, it proves there might still be a story in it for you. Good luck with discovering what it is. I'm going over to the staff block. Irene is going to get suspicious if I don't show my face. This is a rotten job."

He kissed her slowly and regretfully. "I believe you. May I have early morning tea tomorrow, please?"

"Count on it. Enjoy the rest of your evening."

To her surprise, he rubbed his face. "I'm not enjoying it now. This is so odd, Lucy. I've always liked investigations, the knowledge that there's something moving under the surface, the satisfaction in tracking it down. It didn't bother me if it was boring or dangerous. This time... I don't know. I can work on my own, and I can work with you, but working separately and only coming together in furtive bursts..."

He *did* feel the same about this as her. Lucy's heart

was immeasurably eased. She linked her hands behind his head. "We'll send Phoebe home as soon as we can. We'll still be working separately, but at least I won't be lying to your friends."

Jack kissed the tip of her nose. "I don't think that's quite the issue as far as I'm concerned. Forget it, I'm out-of-sorts. Off you go to your blameless rest."

Lucy checked there was nobody about, then watched him stroll towards the main stairs whistling tunefully. She switched off her light, locked the door and headed for the side staircase and the door to the gardens. If she stifled a sigh, hearing the dance music downstairs and the bursts of laughter and the bright hum of conversation, there was no one here to know.

"Miss Brown, Miss Trent, after lunch I shall require you both to work an extra hour on the top floor. The two ladies in suite 37 are now to share room A and their nephew, Lord Elvedon, is to move into room B. The suite will require cleaning throughout and new beds making up." Mrs Ryland contrived to look disapproving as she added, "Your wages will reflect the extra work."

"Yes, Mrs Ryland," said Lucy.

"Nice of her to ask, I don't think," grumbled Irene once the housekeeper was out of earshot. "I might have had plans for my afternoon." It was noticeable, however, that she didn't look as sour as her words implied.

"You and me both," said Lucy. "Myrtle and I are going to the Seagull for lunch. Now I'll get indigestion rushing back." This was a fib. What she had actually been planning was to have lunch as Phoebe as soon as Gustav Karlsson appeared with his picnic basket. It looked as though there were going to be some rapid changes of costume in her future. Even so, it was a piece of luck. Now she would be able to see the lie of the land on the top floor legitimately. She fervently hoped the guests in question would not be present as they must be the bridge-playing aunts she had shared a table with as Phoebe. It would never do to be recognised.

"More developments," she said when she took a tray of early morning tea to Jack and Charles shortly afterwards. "The Earl of Elvedon is joining us in the Bay Sands Hotel."

Charles groaned and buried himself further under the bedclothes.

"Good lord," said Jack, sitting up. "Edward Carter must have even more pull with the management than I suspected. Who have they chucked out?"

He had an endearingly rumpled look and Lucy had to be very strict with herself not to sit on the bed next to him. "No one. He is to share his aunts' suite. Somehow they have been persuaded to give up one of their bedrooms to him and share the other. Astonishing as they were less than thrilled with his company yesterday."

"Carter must have added a sweetener," said Jack thoughtfully. "He's determined to get Rupert for Veronique. What puzzles me is why he wasn't choking off Hilliard harder last night. There has to be something in that. He plays a deep game, does Edward Carter."

"That's for you to work out," said Lucy. "What it means for me is Phoebe won't be at the tennis tournament as early as I'd planned. Irene and I have got to turn around suite 37 first."

"Why you? Why not the top floor chambermaids?"

"One of them has a half-day and the other isn't well. Do you want me to look for anything particular while I'm up there?"

"It would be interesting to know whether Carter's suite or terrace can be accessed apart from through the main door."

Lucy wrinkled her nose. "It's the other end of the corridor from 37, but I'll do my best. See you later." She gave Jack a quick kiss, grateful that Charles was still diplomatically under his blankets, and then took her own tea into Phoebe's room. At least she wouldn't have to do much cleaning in here. She looked wistfully at the undisturbed bed. Would she ever be able to go on a proper holiday with Jack as herself?

The morning moved briskly on. As guests went down for breakfast, she and Irene cleaned the rooms. The sun shone outside and the sea sparkled. It would be a nice day for Gustav Karlsson's picnic. It would be a nice day for the tennis tournament. It would be a really nice day to sit on her balcony and work on her latest detective novel.

Lucy gritted her teeth, put aside unworthy thoughts and mopped up yet another trail of spilt face powder. It had been a shock these last three weeks to see how careless the wealthy were with their cosmetics. She'd said flippantly to Irene that she could have kept herself going for six months on what these women wasted.

Irene had replied that she already did. She had quite a collection of different powders and rouges now. As for lipsticks, sometimes they were thrown away after a single use. One day, she'd added bitterly, she might even have somewhere to go where she could wear them.

Lucy had blinked, but said nothing. After all, she'd retrieved two barely-used lipsticks from guests' waste bins herself to add to Phoebe's make-up bag. Not to wear - she was rather more squeamish than Irene about using something that had been in contact with another person's lips - but to bulk out Phoebe's hastily assembled cosmetic collection. The rest of it had come from the cheap end of her local chemist's counter. Adding verisimilitude, Jack had called it.

It was true though, she mused, as she moved on to

Mr Hilliard's room. People threw away the oddest things. She'd found a pair of cufflinks that had been dropped in the bin one time and had tactfully replaced them on the dressing table. The size of the tip when the guest left had been a nice surprise. There was unlikely to be anything similar in room 1. Mr Hilliard was the tidiest guest she'd ever encountered. Shoes lined up. Clothes hung up or folded away. Book and clock arranged neatly on the bedside table.

Lucy moved the shoes to sweep the carpet and was careful to put them all back as she'd found them. She made the bed, cleaned the bathroom, changed the towels and finally picked up the waste bin to empty it. And stopped. There was a crumpled piece of paper on top with Irene's handwriting on it. As she hesitated, she heard voices outside the door. Lucy slid the scrap of paper into her apron pocket and whisked out with the bin just before Mrs Ryland looked in on her customary round of the rooms.

"Satisfactory, both of you. I shall expect to see you on the top floor after lunch."

The housekeeper turned and Irene rolled her eyes at Lucy behind the starched, unyielding back.

"She's missed her vocation," muttered Lucy once Mrs Ryland was out of earshot. "She should have been a matron in a hospital."

"Maybe she applied and they turned her down for being too strict. I've got one more room to do. See you later."

Myrtle was on the telephone when Lucy, dressed in a boxy jumper and skirt with a blue beret on her dark hair, got to the office. The reception hall was busy with people, so she waited in the switchboard alcove out of the way. It was fascinating listening to the guests' conversations as they sauntered past the counter.

"All I can say, Elvira, is the sooner that young woman persuades him to pop the question the better. The bridge play is reasonable here, but I was hoping to get down to the south coast to the Darlings' house party."

"We'll go at the weekend as planned, Maude. I consider we've more than done our duty. A few judicious comments that she seems a very capable young lady who could run an estate with one hand tied behind her back should do the trick."

"Terribly cold, though."

"She'd hardly be considering him otherwise. That's not our problem. Elvedon is so self-centred he won't notice." She tapped on the counter. "Young man, do you have the railway timetables? Thank you. Now then, Maude, let's see…"

Lucy grinned to herself, then shrank further into the alcove as Mr Hilliard stopped to ask the assistant on duty if there were any letters for him. Hard on his heels came Mr Carter and Gustav Karlsson.

Carter shot a glance at Hilliard, immersed in his post and said, "Are you sure you won't join Mackenzie and Forrest and me for a round on the golf course after lunch? My daughter is going to be tied up with this tennis tournament all afternoon, so we won't have to hurry back."

"Thank you, no. I may take my boat out for a sail. It is beautiful weather for it."

"Another time then." They moved on.

A whirlwind of breathless, leggy twins hurtled down the stairs towards the main entrance. "Daddy! You've arrived! Hello, Jimmy, you're just in time to have lunch and then join us on the tennis court. It's a topping hotel. Masses to do, and just wait until you hear the band."

Mr Lester allowed himself to be greeted enthusiastically

by his daughters, then said, "Lunch sounds most agreeable, but after that I intend to go to my room. Mr Ward may please himself."

"That's all right. You're sharing with Tufty, aren't you, Jimmy? Tufty's playing tennis, so you can too. Gina said she was coming down to watch us."

Mr Ward - a tall, amiable-looking young man - gazed into the middle distance with a faint smile and answered that he'd be happy to.

"Tufty will be jolly glad you're here. He nearly had Rupert Manners as a room mate. Can you imagine?" The girls struck die-away poses with hands to foreheads before collapsing in giggles and heading for the dining room.

Mr Hilliard shuffled his letters together and strolled away. Lucy noticed he'd left one behind, but Myrtle emerged from the office just then, dressed in her outdoor coat and hat and pulling on her gloves.

Lucy ducked around the reception counter and immediately crouched down to re-lace her shoe as Mr Oaks strode out of the Palm Court lounge. He glowered at Mr Ward's departing back and barged roughly past Lord Elvedon's aunts, causing one of them to stagger and cry out in pain, before taking the stairs two at a time.

"Maude, are you all right? Young man, fetch the manager immediately. We wish to lodge a complaint. Appalling manners. Not what one expects in a hotel of this calibre at all."

"Mr Oaks is such a rude man," said Lucy to Myrtle, hurrying her friend through the plate glass doors. "I suppose he got tired of waiting for Miss Bianca and went to hurry her up."

"Mr Oaks?" said Myrtle, her brow wrinkling.

"The man who jostled those women and strode upstairs. He's Miss Bianca's manager or something. He's not staying here."

Myrtle looked back towards the hotel. "Non-residents should only be in the public rooms," she said anxiously. "Maybe I should tell Uncle Faun…"

Lucy grasped her arm. "No, you don't. Once you step back inside, you'll never escape again. Besides, he's already got his comeuppance. The sleeve of his tweed jacket was soaked with spray from the fountain. I saw him in the doorway of the lounge. He must have been standing right next to it." As she spoke, she remembered Gina's dejected air last night and the way she had been crying in her room. "Serve him right. I wouldn't be surprised if he bullies her. He looks the type."

"But Gina Bianca is famous," said Myrtle, shocked.

And fragile. And frightened. "That doesn't stop her being bullied," said Lucy.

"Hello, hello, just the young ladies I was hoping to see," said a jovial voice behind them.

Lucy let Myrtle turn first, pleased that Gustav Karlsson was so prompt. She still had to get back and put in a rapid appearance as Phoebe before turning into Lucy-the-chambermaid again.

"Oh, Mr Karlsson," said Myrtle, blushing rosily.

"What do you think I have here?" he asked, beaming. "A Bay Sands Hotel picnic basket. Would you like to share it?"

He stood there, tall and good-humoured in a seaman's jersey with his cap in his hand and his hair ruffled by the wind. Lucy could feel Myrtle melting with desire.

"I should really get back," she murmured. "I've an extra hour's work after lunch."

"All right," said Myrtle in a faraway voice.

Gustav Karlsson put his peaked cap back on at a jaunty angle, took Myrtle's arm, winked broadly at Lucy and turned in a purposeful manner towards the dunes.

CHAPTER NINE

"I thought you were lunching with Myrtle," said Irene.

Startled, Lucy realised she'd automatically taken the tradesmen's path to the staff block while she worked out a programme of what she had to do next. "I was supposed to," she said. "But she met a friend, so I let them go on without me as I knew I'd have to be back early."

Irene made a sympathetic face. "What a waste of time getting changed. Let's eat quickly, then you can get into uniform afterwards. If we leave it, the bell boys will have finished everything. I swear they've got hollow legs."

That was the first part of the schedule scratched, then. No posh lunch for Phoebe. Lucy followed Irene stoically into the staff dining room.

The top floor, when they got there, was full of purposeful activity. In suite 37, porters moved furniture under Mrs Ryland's directions. Lucy and Irene transferred belongings, cleaned the vacated room and made up the bed. Lucy was sent along to the chambermaid's cubby for clean bedding for the twin room.

"I don't see why I shouldn't wear it at the cocktail party tonight," said Veronique Carter's slightly petulant voice from further along the corridor.

"It will make more impact at the grand ball," replied

her father. "Here is the lift. Enjoy your tennis tournament, my dear. I may be back for tea, depending on when we finish playing golf."

"Must be nice to have too many clothes to wear," muttered Irene in her ear. "Have they gone? Shall we have a nose in her suite?"

"We can't," said Lucy, though she was dying to.

"Come on, we'll say we got lost."

But though the door to Miss Carter's suite was open when they walked along the passage with their armloads of bedding, her maid could be clearly seen fluffing up the cushions in the sitting room. The door to Mr Carter's suite was firmly closed, as were the others along the corridor.

Irene shrugged. "It was worth a try."

"We'll have to use our imagination," agreed Lucy.

"Miss Trent, Miss Brown," called Mrs Ryland.

They exchanged a look and sped back.

"Did the bedding require two pairs of arms?" asked the housekeeper acidly. "Once you have made the beds *one* of you will have to fetch a second ashtray for this room."

"Yes, Mrs Ryland," said Lucy seeing the afternoon tick away even more.

There were no spare ashtrays in the cubby, so rather than request one from maintenance, Lucy pelted down to her own floor. At the top of the side stairs, however, an arm shot out and caught hold of her.

"Take care," said the owner of the arm in a resonant Russian-accented voice. "It is not safe to run on these stairs."

Her heart thudding with shock, Lucy thanked the waiter and proceeded at a more decorous pace. From the delay before she heard the upper door close, she guessed he'd been watching her to make sure she obeyed. She supposed it was nice of him to be concerned, but she bristled inwardly just the same.

She quickly collected an ashtray and started back up. On entering the stairwell, she heard a scrabbling sound and a closing door from above but when she looked up, there was no one there. *Less haste, more speed,* she reminded herself and ascended circumspectly. It was just as well. Halfway up, she spotted a loose skein of fishing line lying just where an unwary step might have sent her skidding.

"One of the guests being careless again," she muttered. "Expecting us to clear up after them the whole time." She stowed it in her apron pocket feeling virtuous.

"She's passed us," said Irene when she got back. "Come on, let's clear off."

"My poor legs," said Lucy with a groan as they once more entered the stairwell.

Irene gave a small cry as a dark shape loomed up.

"Sorry, miss." The waiter hurried past her with a bottle of gin in his hand.

"Oh, he did startle me," said Irene.

"They're all over the stairs this afternoon," said Lucy. "Setting up for the cocktail party, I expect."

"He's lucky I didn't make him drop the bottle. At the Savoy, that would have been taken out of his wages *and* he'd have had to work an extra hour."

"How awful. At least conditions are better here, even if it's not so lively. You carry on. I'm just going to have a word with Myrtle."

She watched Irene hurry across the grass to the staff block. Now to finally change into Phoebe for what remained of the afternoon.

Having lost his early matches with considerable artistry, Jack was watching the onlookers for a sight of Lucy. At last, the pink and white figure of Phoebe Sugar appeared on the cocktail terrace with her camera. He found himself smiling as she picked her way carefully down the steps.

"I missed you at lunch," he murmured as she lined up for an action shot of Charles and Veronique, currently destroying Theo Nicholson and Julie Lester.

"Don't," she said. "Just don't. We are going to have to send Phoebe home. This isn't about lying to your friends any more, I simply can't keep going at this pace. I nearly came out just now in my working shoes. There's no point Phoebe being here anyway. You and Charles are monitoring the guests and I see more behind the scenes as a chambermaid."

"Phoebe will have to stay for the ball," pointed out Jack. "And it does mean we can talk more often. How was the top floor?"

"Aside from Mrs Ryland's idea of an hour's work not being the same as mine and Irene's, it was busy like you wouldn't believe. The back staircase is full of Russians popping in and out of the landings with chairs and bottles. I didn't have any luck with either of the Carter suites. Mr Carter's door was shut. Grigory and his waiters are now setting up in Miss Carter's sitting room for her cocktail party. I did manage to stroll out of the balcony door in suite 37 while we were sprucing. There are decorative waist-high railings separating all the roof terraces, so I don't see how your eavesdropper managed to get to where you saw him without being seen himself. Oh, and Mrs Portman was entertaining someone in her suite. They'd left the blinds open. Irene thought the man was one of the croupiers. I didn't look closely enough to be able to tell."

"I should think not. What would your mother say."

"I imagine she'd be speechless. You might have a better chance wandering around the other end of the terraces this evening."

"I can but try. Well played," he called as Veronique, flushed with triumph, smashed home the winning shot.

"Is the tournament finished?" asked Lucy.

"Not yet. That was the first doubles semi-final. Next on are Amanda and Hubert versus Tufty Thomas and Jimmy Ward. Jimmy's a demon. He has the absent-minded air of someone who's working out the compound interest on a foreign investment in his head, and then he slams in an ace with deadly accuracy. It's going down a storm with Gina Bianca."

Lucy glanced across to where Gina was sitting with a lively group, sipping an iced drink and laughing. "Gosh," she said. "What a change. You'd think she'd never sobbed herself ugly behind a closed door in her life."

"I imagine the absence of the ape-like Mr Oaks is at least partly responsible."

"Has he disappeared again? I saw him going up the stairs before lunch looking like thunder, so perhaps they've had a row. Has Gina been playing tennis herself?"

"No, she's hurt her shoulder. Take another photo and then let's stroll around to have a look at the bay. I feel like consoling myself with a little light flirtation."

"You say the nicest things. Don't you have to play again?"

"I am happy to report that I lost my singles and my doubles matches with a great deal of ingenuity. Thus I am free to go and lick my wounds with a pretty girl."

"That's a really unsavoury image, Jack."

"Don't tell me you don't want to breathe in some sea air to chase away the carbolic."

She grinned sideways at him. "I daresay I could be tempted."

He had to stop himself taking her arm as they walked around the outside of the hotel. "This is positively the last time we do a job where we pretend not to know each other," he said. "It's playing havoc with my natural impulses."

"The sooner you find out what is going on here the

better then." Lucy looked towards the golf course. "Over there is where you should have been this afternoon, not losing cleverly at tennis. Mr Carter and Mr Mackenzie and Mr Forrest are playing golf. Didn't you once say golf was about business, not pleasure?"

"At their level it is. I did suggest I ought to get in a round while I'm here and was given a brush off with a strong hint that attendance at the tennis tournament was not voluntary. They are probably discussing building a new pier for Rupert's theatre and buying up the rest of Kingsthorpe. I only wish I knew why. It can't just be that Edward Carter has a nostalgic fondness for the place."

"Stranger things have happened. Maybe he wants somewhere to call his own."

"Whose side are you on? There's no story in that for me." He glanced around. "Is it my imagination or are there an awful lot of gardeners manicuring the lawns and flower beds at the back of this hotel?"

"Two of the new intake are gardeners, according to Myrtle. They are here to stop idle playboys seducing hard-working columnists by way of a quick canoodle in the rhododendron bushes."

Jack looked down at her fondly as they rounded the corner. "I don't suppose I could interest you in a secluded sand dune instead?"

But Lucy had stopped. "Ordinarily yes," she said in an odd voice. "Probably not today."

She was trembling. "What is it?" said Jack in concern. "What's wrong. Tell me."

She nodded at something in front of them. "Look."

Jack looked. And swore softly. Just beyond the sharp corner of the hotel, Xavier Hilliard lay sprawled across the path. Like Jack, he was wearing tennis whites. Unlike Jack, he had made contact with the ground with considerable force.

"Hell," said Jack. The lover was gone. The dallying playboy was gone. His mind filled with all the things that needed to happen in the next few minutes, the next few hours, the next few days. It was like a tidal surge of jobs to be done, racing in to the exclusion of all else. "Get a photograph," he said as a first step. "Take it now."

"No! It's ghoulish and I'm not that sort of journalist. I may write mystery stories, but I can invent perfectly competent gory details without needing to study them closely myself. As for Phoebe, she simply tells the public who has been seen dancing with who and what fashionable women are wearing this season."

"Not for the paper, Lucy, for Uncle Bob. Hilliard had enemies, plus I'm damned sure he was up to something here. Whether he fell or whether he was pushed, photographs will be evidence. The local police might do it, but only if I can stop Fauntleroy Delaney tidying the body away to an empty storeroom before they get here. I'll ring them straight away and I'll break the news to Delaney that he now has a spare room. If I'm any judge, he'll be around in twenty seconds to cover him up and save the guests' sensibilities."

There was something else he should take care of, distasteful though it was. He moved forward and rapidly felt in Hilliard's pockets.

"What are you doing?" hissed Lucy.

"Taking charge of his keys, his wallet and any other personal possessions. We can't leave them lying around for unscrupulous people to help themselves."

"You are the height of honesty, of course," said Lucy tartly. "Move out of the way unless you want to be in the photograph. This is horrible, Jack."

"Half a minute." He stood away from the body, tucking Hilliard's belongings into the inside pocket of his blazer. "He's cool, but not cold. It can't have happened long ago.

I wonder how far he fell?" He looked up at the roof, at the balconies. At Lucy's balcony at the end of the row. It was directly above them. He felt his heart move in protest.

"What is it?" she asked.

"Nothing. Will you be all right staying here while I inform Delaney and try to get through to the Yard? Uncle Bob told us to look for anything suspicious, and if this isn't suspicious, then I don't know what is. He'll want to send someone along to Hilliard's office as soon as I get word to him. Xavier had fingers in many pies."

"I'll be fine, but do hurry. Don't say anything on the phone that you don't want Florence on the switchboard to hear. Use the callbox at the garage if you have to."

That's my grand girl. He kissed her swiftly. "You think I'm an amateur? We have a code. I'll be as quick as I can."

Alone, Lucy made a resolute effort and looked at Mr Hilliard. It was no use being squeamish. She had understood Jack's glance at her balcony, though quite why Hilliard would be up there if he was supposed to be playing tennis she had no idea. However, if she herself wasn't to be asked too many awkward questions about her presence here, they would have to garner as much information as possible while they still could. She swallowed, focusing the camera. It wasn't easy. Tidy dead bodies in hospital beds were one thing. Lucy had got used to those when she was nursing at the convalescent hospital during the war. This was altogether messier.

Then she caught her breath. Mr Hilliard was wearing his white shoes with the thin crepe soles. She had seen those shoes this morning. They had been as clean as a whistle, both on top and underneath.

Now one sole was smeared with something white. Had he walked on something slippery? Chalk, perhaps?

It didn't look quite right, but Lucy suspected she wasn't thinking straight. She crouched and took a photograph of the shoes, purely on instinct, then moved on to full length shots from three different angles. For the rest of her life she would associate the faint scent of lavender in the air with the fierce concentration of taking photos of surface details and closing her mind to the body.

She was sitting on a stylish modern bench staring resolutely out to sea by the time Mr Delaney and two of the waiters puffed up wearing appalled expressions and carrying a snowy white restaurant tablecloth.

"This is dreadful. What a terrible accident to befall one of our guests. Cover him, Feodor, quickly. The ladies' sensibilities… they must not be upset by such an unfortunate sight. My dear Miss Sugar, you must rest in the lounge immediately, with cognac for the shock, and strong coffee. Feodor, you will see to it. Grigory is bringing a stretcher. Hurry him along."

It was evident that Mr Delaney was determined to move his embarrassingly dead guest out of the way. Lucy took a shaky breath. "I think… that is, Mr Sinclair said you would not want to disturb anything before the police have been."

Police. She could feel the word exploding into him. The waiters stiffened. Mr Delaney looked fixedly into the middle distance. "A groundsheet," he said at last. "And raised planks as if we are doing paving work. Feodor, ask Pyotr to organise this. It must look as though there is nothing to see. Mr Sinclair is correct. One should not obstruct the police."

"I am sure you are doing the right thing," said Lucy as the first waiter hurried away.

Mr Delaney was still thinking. "Refreshments for the tennis party," he said, snapping his fingers. "Ah, Grigory, there you are. We have a change of plan. We must leave the unfortunate man here to await the police. Take extra refreshments to the tennis courts. A charming alfresco picnic. That will keep everyone at the back of the hotel."

They went into a huddled colloquy. Lucy kept the mound of Hilliard's body in the corner of her vision, but remained with her back to the staff. She didn't at all trust Grigory's sharp eyes not to penetrate her disguise. It was with considerable relief that she heard Jack's voice.

"The police are on their way, Mr Delaney," he said in a tone that indicated he had helped the manager out as a matter of duty, but would prefer to now continue with his holiday.

Lucy listened with appreciation as he suggested in a noble voice that he could join Miss Sugar on the bench until the police arrived, if Mr Delaney himself wished to return inside. Mr Delaney's assistant, he added, seemed to be rather flustered, though no doubt he was doing his best.

Within moments they had the bench to themselves. Jack patted her hand awkwardly as a small group of gardeners arrived with planks and a tarpaulin. She shaded her eyes as if overwrought.

The waiter paused by the bench. "You would like coffee, madam? Sir?"

"Thank you," said Jack. "Most welcome."

"Did you get through?" she breathed as soon as the waiter had gone.

"Yes. He's going to pull strings. Probably means he'll be on the next train if I know him."

"Jack, I've been thinking. I'm going to need to be Lucy in a couple of hours. Am I going to be able to get to my bedroom to change?"

"Oh lord, I was forgetting. I don't know. It's possible all the rooms at the sharp end will be examined for prints. I suggest you go up now, hide your uniform in my room just in case, and come back. As the people who found the body, we can create enough fuss to give our story straight away, then you can say you need to rest. No one will doubt you feeling ill after a shock like this."

Lucy nodded, smiled bravely at him and went inside. Her room appeared to be as she'd left it. She transferred her uniform to beneath the covers in Jack's bed next door, put her working shoes at the back of his wardrobe and returned.

"I didn't go on to the balcony and I only touched the bare minimum," she said, sipping the coffee that had arrived in her absence. "It didn't look as though anyone had been in there. I can't help wishing Phoebe had stayed in London. You realise if they take my fingerprints for elimination purposes my dual identity will be exposed."

"Uncle Bob got you into this. He can get you out."

"Is he sure he'll be brought in? Scotland Yard have to be sent for. My books are full of devices to ensure the local force bumble along on their own, leaving it to gifted amateurs to solve the crime."

Jack ticked off the reasons on his fingers. "Hilliard was based in London. Delaney's previous hotel was in London. Most of the guests have London addresses as well as country ones. The reason we are here in the first place is because Uncle Bob has his eye on the Bay Sands Hotel. Curtis of the Yard will be here within the next three hours, I guarantee it."

His logic was soothing, but Lucy still felt apprehensive. "I suppose so. And lo, I see a police car approaching."

CHAPTER TEN

What a thing to happen, bewailed Delaney to himself. What a thing to happen at the Bay Sands Hotel. Now the constabulary would be here, upsetting his residents, prowling through his beautiful rooms. And a private cocktail party taking place in suite 42 in a few hours and then the grand ball tomorrow. He daren't even think about what Mr Carter and the other owners would say when they came back from the golf course to find the police on the premises. It was enough to make a man despair.

However, he was doing what he could. Pyotr would screen Xavier Hilliard's body from all eyes. Feodor would soothe the two guests who had stumbled across him. Grigory would keep the tennis players and onlookers near the courts. Perhaps, thought Delaney hopefully, the police would conclude it was an accident, remove him and go away before anyone realised what had happened.

At this juncture, Delaney was seized by justifiable fury. Why, if Xavier Hilliard had wanted to throw himself off a tall building - and heaven knows there must be enough people willing to give him a hand - had he not made use of his perfectly adequate office window in Harley Street? Why had he put himself to the trouble of a train journey to Kingsthorpe, disturbing Delaney's peace and making impossible demands about moving to a different room, before adding insult to injury by wrecking his lovely ambience and bringing the police down on him?

Alive, Hilliard had been incalculable, smooth as silk, persistent in worming out every irregularity that he could turn to advantage, and very dangerous. Dead, he had the potential to be much worse. Delaney needed sympathy and busy efficiency. He went into Myrtle's office in search of them.

His niece was staring dreamily into space.

It was as if the bottom had dropped out of his world. Her abstraction was almost more shocking than the discovery of a dead moneylender outside his hotel. "Myrtle!" he said in consternation.

"Hello, Uncle Faun, did you want something?"

Delaney pulled himself together. "I... yes. Mr Hilliard has met with a most unfortunate accident. A fall. A fatal one. The police will be here shortly. It's a terrible thing to happen at the hotel. Terrible."

Myrtle was satisfyingly solicitous. She jumped up and patted his hand and agreed that it was shocking but she knew he would manage.

"It's a pity he didn't pay in advance," she said. "Still, we'll easily be able to re-book his room so it's only a loss of a few nights."

"As long as there is no..." Delaney paused and lowered his voice. "Publicity."

There was a knock on the door. "The police," said Delaney's assistant in a hushed voice.

Delaney glanced through the clouded glass and shuddered at the sight of massive blue uniforms in his stylish hotel reception. "Gentlemen," he said, hurrying out to them. "My name is Delaney. I'm the manager. Do come through to my office."

"Much obliged," said the older of the policemen.

"Sergeant Pine. We met when I had a little look-see at your casino when you applied for the licence. If it's all the same to you, sir, I think we'd better view the body first."

Delaney dropped his voice to a reverent murmur, hoping they would take the hint. "Certainly, certainly. This way." He led them outside and watched in some anxiety as the policemen lifted the tarpaulin and looked in silence at Hilliard. "If you wish to use the telephone to arrange for him to be taken to the mortuary, just say the word." *As soon as possible, please.*

"Thank you, sir. If I might phone the superintendent..." said Sergeant Pine. He stepped back, leaving his constable to replace the covering.

"Of course." He stopped in a distracted manner by the bench where Mr Sinclair had risen with well-bred impatience. "These are the hotel guests who found him."

"Glad to meet you. If you'll give your names and addresses and a description of the incident to Constable Williams, that will be helpful," said the sergeant, and continued into the hotel.

Delaney waited outside his own office while the sergeant used the telephone. So good was the soundproofing that he couldn't hear a word of the conversation. Normally, this would have gratified him.

The sergeant came out looking impassive. "Well now, it seems we'll be with you for a little while. Purely routine. Is there a room we could use to take statements and such like?"

"Of course," said Delaney unhappily, leading him across to the other side of the grand staircase and hoping the small sitting room was vacant. "What sort of statements?"

"Those guests outside who found him. Anyone who talked to him this afternoon. I daresay the staff will be able to help."

Delaney stared at him in horror. "But that means you'll want to talk to everyone."

"It won't take long. Most people won't come into the picture at all," replied Sergeant Pine with unimpaired good humour. He sat down at the writing table and got out a notebook. "For example, when did you last see the deceased?"

"After lunch. I noticed him ascending the stairs."

"Was he dressed as he is now?"

"Naturally not, he was in a lounge suit. He would have been going up to change for tennis."

Sergeant Pine beamed. "There. And I've no doubt his opponent can get us that bit further with his movements. You see? Purely routine."

"It was a tournament," said Delaney wretchedly. "A number of guests are taking part in it. They are down there still." *Including Miss Carter. Including the Earl of Elvedon.* Mentally, Delaney wept and beat his bosom.

"Ah, said Sergeant Pine, scratching his chin, "that does put rather a different complexion on things, yes. What a good thing Constable Williams brought a spare notebook."

Lucy gave her statement to the younger policeman along with Jack, and then went upstairs. It didn't seem to have occurred to Sergeant Pine to put the bedrooms out of bounds, so this was as good an opportunity as she was likely to get to turn back into herself. She would lock her camera away and sit in the cubby for a while. If Mrs Ryland asked why she was on duty early, she had the excuse of natural curiosity. Judging by the way all the waiters and reception staff were buzzing with the news, there was no chance that it hadn't reached the staff block.

It was an unpleasant shock, as she came around the corner from the main staircase, to see a chambermaid closing the door of room 1 and disappearing down the side stairs.

Irene. That was her immediate thought, followed by genuine astonishment that Sergeant Pine hadn't sealed Mr Hilliard's room. It was the sort of mistake the police in her mysteries made, but she'd assumed she'd invented it herself. She hadn't realised it happened in real life. Jack's uncle was going to have a few words to say about that for sure.

Her second thought, following slowly and reluctantly, was *Why was Irene in there?* She had an idea, but she couldn't be sure. Quickly, she let herself into Jack's room to retrieve her uniform.

Seconds later, the door opened, causing her heart to leap into her throat. It was Jack himself. She breathed again.

"Charles is on his way up," he said. "Have you got time for a résumé?"

Lucy nodded. "As soon as I've changed. Did you know Mr Hilliard's room isn't sealed?"

"Oh ye gods and little fishes," said Jack in an exasperated voice. "How do these people sleep at night? Sergeant Pine probably thinks because he's got the key, nobody can get in. I'll see if I can suggest it without giving offence."

He dashed out. Lucy returned to her own room. It wouldn't be long before the tennis players came upstairs to bathe and change. A person could hear a surprising amount sitting quietly out of sight or walking around with an armful of towels.

As she tied the apron there was a crackle from her pocket. Biting her lip in worry, her hand went to the scrap of paper she'd found in Mr Hilliard's waste bin this morning. Another complication. And something else had just occurred to her that she ought to discuss with Jack.

On the thought, she heard his soft tap on her door and slipped out to join him and Charles in the next room. "The *Chronicle*," she said, coming straight to the point, "is not going to be happy if I don't at least mention this in passing along with the latest sports styles worn by the smart set to play tennis."

"I thought you said Phoebe wasn't that sort of reporter."

"She isn't, but neither is she blind, deaf or dumb. And she *found* the body, Jack. Her credibility will drop through the floor if she doesn't let them know. I wondered about phoning through something like *'Tragedy marred the eve of the official opening ball at the Bay Sands Hotel in Kingsthorpe when one of the guests fell to his death from a balcony. The balconies had previously been inspected by the fire service and pronounced safe. It is the first incident of its kind since the hotel opened its doors to guests seven months ago. There was a minute's silence before dinner as a mark of respect.'* What do you think?"

"Very discreet in the circumstances," said Jack.

"The point being that I mention it, but without any names. If they want more, I'll tell them the police asked me to withhold details until the relatives can be informed."

Jack nodded. "Good solution. What have you got, Charles?"

"A couple of things, both of which could be important," said Charles. He was reclining against his pillows, still wearing his tennis gear. Lucy wondered how long it would be before the urge to tick people off for disarranging bed coverings left her.

Jack wasn't disarranging anything, bless him. He was sitting tidily at the table writing notes. "Go on," he said.

"I was pouring out a glass of fruit cup for my regrettably triumphant partner - really, Veronique is not a graceful winner - when one of the waiters hurried down and called out in Russian to our friend Pyotr."

"So much for discretion," said Jack.

"He said that the wolf was dead and Pyotr was to bring a tarpaulin to the path in front of the hotel. Pyotr stared and repeated *'the front?'* in tones of astonishment. The waiter said that was right and he didn't understand either. The impression I got was that they were unsurprised by the death, but puzzled as to the location."

"Well now," said Jack. "That *is* interesting. As if they were expecting something to happen?"

"That was my conclusion."

"They definitely called him the wolf?"

"Oh yes. They knew him."

"One rather wonders how."

"I can ask Myrtle if he has been here before," said Lucy. "I want to know how her lunch with Mr Karlsson went anyway." She glanced at Jack's bedside clock. "It'll have to be tomorrow. She'll have gone home by now."

"You said a couple of things, Charles. What else?"

"Reactions. When the police came down to ask who Hilliard had been playing tennis with - which was no one - they also wanted to know whether anyone had wandered off during the tournament, gone for a walk, gone back to the hotel etc. Certain people cut up rough about the questions, demanding to know why they were being asked, so Sergeant Pine eventually let on that Hilliard was not only late for the tournament, but late altogether. Upon which, Gina Bianca slid into a dead faint."

"Good lord."

"She *said* it was because someone had knocked her bad shoulder, but I have my doubts as Jimmy was standing right next to her in that absent-mindedly protective way he has. The only other person who looked anything other than conventionally shocked was Mrs Lester. It was only for a fraction of a second, but she definitely had an expression of racing calculation on her face."

Jack wrote busily, then walked over to the window. "I'd love to take a good look at these balconies, but we've been told not to use them. There's a lone constable on the jetty keeping a watch to make sure people obey."

Lucy snorted. "So I heard. Judging by the comments from the guests, they are more put out by that than by the death. Jack, won't it be awkward if it is your uncle on the case? Won't people think you might be spying on them for him?"

Jack exchanged a look with Charles. "I doubt they'll realise we are related. I wouldn't be able to get away with it at home with everyone in the county knowing people's bloodlines back to the Conqueror, but I don't think people here will make the association. The thing about this crowd, the shifting, seasonal gaiety-seekers, is that it's shallow. I'm a Sinclair. There are a lot of us. My father had seven siblings. I've got two brothers and two sisters myself. If anyone does happen to recall one of my mother's brothers joining the police force twenty years ago, well, we just say he disapproves of my extravagant lifestyle, so we rarely acknowledge each other in public."

Lucy was appalled. Her family might drive her to distraction, but she couldn't imagine ever pretending they didn't exist. "Doesn't that hurt?" The words were out before she could stop them.

"Sacrifices for the greater good," murmured Charles.

Jack said nothing.

Lucy swallowed. "It's time I was getting back to my cubby. I'll see what else I can overhear."

She went into the corridor, trying not to think about Jack letting himself appear so much less than he was in order to fight crime his own way. The two ladies sharing room 3 came up the stairs and passed her, talking about the tennis. They didn't even give the room beyond them a glance as they went inside.

Didn't know him, didn't care. Lucy was suddenly profoundly dejected. She sat down, thinking what a long evening it was going to be. There was movement in the doorway. Irene stood there, her hands working.

"Hello," said Lucy. "You've heard the news then. Isn't it terrible?"

"Shocking," said Irene. "I thought you might need a hand."

"You are such a bad liar, Irene. How long had you been acquainted with Mr Hilliard?"

Her friend turned pale. "You knew?" she whispered.

Lucy drew the piece of paper out of her pocket and smoothed it on her apron. There were six words on it. *People in room all the time.*

"Oh, thank God," said Irene, collapsing into the chair next to her with relief.

"It was in his waste paper basket this morning. I recognised your writing." Lucy passed the scrap to Irene who took a box of matches from her pocket and shakily set the message alight in the ashtray.

"I came up here to search for it as soon as I heard. I knew it wouldn't look good. When I couldn't find it, I thought he'd have it on him. It would be just like him. I've been sick with nerves. Me!"

In the ashtray, the last flame licked across the corner of the paper and died. Just for a moment, the word *time* was illuminated in red spider writing, then it was gone, a smudge of grey ash. "Do you want to tell me about it?" asked Lucy.

Irene gave her a long look. "You're very trusting. How do you know I didn't push him?"

"Well, aside from the fact you were with me most of the early afternoon..."

"I was forgetting. All right, why not? It goes back to when I had to borrow money for Ma's medicine. I was working two jobs to pay it off, neither of them any good. Cleaning at the Commercial and usher at the picture house. One evening a few months ago the main picture had just started when this man Hilliard turns up. Smooth as butter and twice as slippery. Didn't know him from Adam. I was going to show him to a seat, but he stops me and says he wants a word first. Says he knows who I am and that he's bought up my debt from old Solomon. He said he'd cancel it if I did him a favour."

"What sort of a favour?"

"Not that," said Irene with a dry look. "Once bitten, twice shy where that's concerned, I promise you. It was the Bay Sands Hotel. It was just being fitted out. Hilliard told me to chuck the Commercial and get a chambermaid job here as soon as they advertised. Then I was to tell him the set up and steal him a pass key to all the rooms. He said if I did that, he'd give me the docket back. I'd be free of debt."

"That's all? Too good to be true."

"Beggars can't be choosers. I suppose it wasn't a lot of money to him, however much it is to me. I told him I wasn't born yesterday, and I wouldn't write anything down. I'd phone him and reverse the charges. He said that was fine and gave me his office number. I met him in a tea shop in Kingsthorpe the day he arrived and gave him the key. I don't know why he wanted it and I didn't ask. Don't look at me like that. Until you've been in debt yourself with the interest ticking up faster than you can pay it back, you don't know what you'd do to get out."

"I'm not judging," said Lucy.

"I was surprised when he called me into room 1 yesterday morning. He'd *said* he wanted one of the rooms up at the sharp end."

My room. "Maybe he didn't book early enough and someone else got in first."

"Yeah. Anyway, he showed me the ticket with the debt half-cancelled. He said he'd write off the rest at the end of his stay, because there might be more he wanted me to do for him. Twisty bastard."

"Did he keep it on him?" *Because Jack had handed over his wallet and pocket book to Sergeant Pine...*

A stubborn look crossed Irene's ace. "No. It was buttoned into the inside pocket of his overcoat. That was the other thing I was looking for. I burnt it as soon as I got back to my room. You wouldn't believe the relief."

"I can imagine it. What a weight off your mind. Did he want you to do anything else?"

"He asked who was in room 19. That was easy because you said Miss Sugar was working in there, so I went straight back and told him. Then he wanted to know who was on the top floor apart from the Carters. I said how would I know that? The only guest I knew about was Mrs Portman because of the girls telling us about her and because she took Alex the pro dancer up there on Monday night and Olga was spitting venom at him all through breakfast."

"She was," agreed Lucy. "Russian is a tremendous language to swear in. Did Mr Hilliard ask about anything else?"

"Later he wanted me to find out if the Carters' suites were ever unattended. I had to fake an excuse to get up there when I went off-duty and of course they weren't. That valet and Miss Carter's maid and one of the secretaries were eating there. I overheard the secretary say he'd got orders to stay until Mr Carter returned. That's what the note was about."

"Did you find anything else when you were looking for your debt? Any other papers?" *Ease off, Lucy, or she's going to want to know why you are interested.*

Irene looked puzzled. "No. Why?"

Lucy shrugged. "I just wondered, that's all. If he had something on you, he might have had something on other people as well."

"Bound to have done, he was that sort, but I expect he

keeps everything in a safe in his office. He only brought mine to wave in front of my face. Like I say, it would have been small change to him. Did you see his clothes? They weren't bought off a market stall, were they?"

Lucy took a deep breath. "I think you should tell the police."

Irene half-stood in alarm. "Are you mad? Present them with a motive? I was in debt to him. I might as well march myself into a cell at the station and throw away the key."

"What if he's left a record back in his office? What if he's got a duplicate of your debt?"

"What if he hasn't?"

"You're alibied, Irene. We were changing suite 37 together, then I watched you go across to the staff wing before I tried to get a word with Myrtle. Letting the police know the situation will tell them Mr Hilliard was after something. It will tell them he wasn't just here to enjoy himself. They'll find out anyway, so getting in with them before you have to has got to be a good idea."

Irene looked mulish. "I'll think about it. They're still interviewing guests at the moment."

Lucy stood and peered out into the corridor. "Think fast then. It won't take them long to get around to checking up on the staff. I won't mention the note. That's between you and me and I've forgotten it already. Just tell them about the debt."

"You're a real bully," complained Irene, but there was no heat in her words. She stood up, went to the doorway, then looked back. "I don't suppose you've got a nip of gin in your apron pocket?"

"Sorry."

"Collect my wages and take it to Ma if I get clapped into jug, okay?"

"They won't arrest you, Irene."

"What if they tell Mr Delaney? I don't want to lose

this job, whatever I might say about it. It pays twice what I was getting at the Commercial."

"Why would they? They just want the facts. The fact is, Mr Hilliard had an ulterior motive for being here that was strong enough for him to go to the trouble of looking up local moneylenders and buying up useful debts."

Irene sighed. "When you put it like that... I'll think about it a bit harder. See you at supper."

"Save me a space."

CHAPTER ELEVEN

Jack was once again sitting on a bench outside the Bay Sands Hotel when a sandy-haired gentleman with keen eyes and an air of mild authority alighted from a car. He was carrying a leather bag reminiscent of a doctor's case. With him was another gentleman, taller, blockier, slightly older. They could have passed anywhere for a couple of businessmen. The car drove away.

"Good evening," said the first gentleman to Jack, glancing without comment at the tarpaulin-covered arrangement of planks at the far end of the building. "I wonder if you could tell me where the manager of this hotel is to be found?"

"On the top floor at a cocktail party where I ought to be," replied Jack. "It isn't going with quite such a swing as it might, due to the roof terrace having a barricade of chairs along the edge at the insistence of the local police. If you prefer an area where feelings are a little less fraught, might I recommend the first small sitting room on your left as you cross the foyer. It contains Sergeant Pine of the Kingsthorpe constabulary, a most dogged and diligent officer."

"Very useful. Thank you. And where will you be for the next hour?"

"Changing for dinner in room 17, where I may be joined by a chambermaid if my luck is in. You are welcome to make one of the party."

"How kind." Both men nodded genially and went inside. Jack waited for a few minutes, then he too crossed the plush reception carpet before making his way upstairs. Lucy was in her cubby, reading a picture paper.

"Hello," he said. "I thought you'd be finished by now. Shouldn't Phoebe be dressing for dinner?"

"Phoebe is suffering from belated shock and has lost her appetite," replied Lucy. "I'm going back to the staff wing."

Jack looked at her shrewdly. "Arm yourself with a resigned expression and come and tell me why. We should have plenty of time before Curtis of the Yard is ready to do his stuff."

"It is him, then?"

"Was it ever in doubt?" He listened to what she'd found out from Irene and agreed with her conclusions.

"I have to be over there," she finished. "Whether she'll want to talk or not, she might want company and it would be really hurtful if I seemed to ignore her just when she's opened up to me."

Jack was far from being as sanguine about Lucy's friend as she was, but he couldn't question her judgement of a woman she'd been working with day in, day out, for three weeks. "Be very careful, Lucy. Don't give yourself away, but keep your ears open for anyone who may be discussing Hilliard's death."

"Irene said they all are. The Russians are terrifically agitated, all muttering together in huddles."

Jack made a disgruntled noise. "And they called Hilliard 'the wolf' and weren't surprised at his death. It's a pity there isn't a way for Charles to listen in on them. Much as I hate to admit it, you are right to go. I imagine all the staff will be visited by Uncle Bob and Inspector Maynard some time this evening to answer questions."

"That was also in my mind. Let's hope the police don't have an aversion to red flannel dressing gowns."

At that moment, Jack would willingly have swapped all the Paris couture likely to be on display downstairs for a homely flannel dressing gown. Glumly, he laid out his dress suit on the bed and waited for his uncle to discover the first floor.

"Evening, Jack. No chambermaids?"

"Hello, Uncle Bob. Nice to see you again, Inspector Maynard. No, her shift is over and she thought she would be less conspicuous in the staff wing."

"Pity. I wanted her to tell me whether Hilliard's room was as she saw it last."

"I daresay you can send someone to fetch her. She's expecting a visitation from you. Ask to see both the first floor chambermaids. I'm not sure the rest of the staff will be quite as overjoyed by your presence."

"None of them saw anything, according to Sergeant Pine," said Inspector Maynard. "Not that we expected any different."

"That doesn't surprise me. Do you want my notes?"

"Please. I also want to sort out the terrain in my head. Thank you for the prompt call. We got a team to Hilliard's Harley Street office straight away, but someone had beaten us to it. Lock had been forced. Drawer contents untidy. However, the safe was intact, so we are getting the keys down there to see what secrets it holds. Meanwhile, a very thorough inspection is being made of Hilliard's paperwork."

"The office was broken into? That was quick," said Jack. "Meaning someone up here has contacted someone down there?"

"That's one explanation."

"Good lord." Jack straightened his tie in the mirror, thinking about the implications.

"Go and sup your consommé. Give me your notes. I'll find you when I want you."

"Where are you staying?"

"The Resplendent. Maynard and I dropped Fenn and Draper there to sort out rooms and see about hiring a car. They'll be here shortly to take photographs and go over the place for prints. Mr Delaney is devastated that he is unable to accommodate us until Hilliard's room is released."

Jack chuckled. "I can imagine." He pointed out Xavier Hilliard's room and Lucy's room, then strolled down the main stairs in search of dinner.

A gaggle of merry young men were there, including Theo and Hubert. "Where have you been?" said Theo. "You missed the cocktails."

Jack made a rueful face. "I was summoned. Tecs from the Yard have arrived. They wanted my story all over again. Beginning to wish I hadn't stumbled across the blighter."

Tufty stared at him owlishly. "It's a judgement on you for sliding away from the tennis for a woo with that photographer female and not staying for the whole tournament."

"Expect she'll hate the sight of you now, Jack. She'll associate you with dead bodies. Serve you right."

"Who's been teaching you psychology, Hubert?"

"Well, where is she then, eh?"

"Resting," said Jack. "Shock."

Theo shook his head. "That's her story. Lucky Jack Sinclair finally loses his touch. It's a sad day."

"Tragic," agreed Hubert. "We'll give you a hand drowning your sorrows, Jack."

They went in to dinner amidst much hilarity. Jack came

to the conclusion that cocktails were a much overrated way of passing a pre-prandial hour.

"Miss Brown? Miss Trent? I'm told you are the chambermaids responsible for the first floor."

"Yes, sir." Lucy looked respectfully at Inspector Maynard, just as if she hadn't spent an hour with him in Jack's uncle's office being thoroughly briefed on the sort of things to watch out for behind the scenes before starting this job.

"We wondered if you'd both mind telling us how Mr Hilliard's room looked the last time you saw it, and when that was."

In a corner of the room, the younger of the uniformed policemen was taking notes. Presumably Chief Inspector Curtis was interviewing a different set of people with Sergeant Pine. Lucy devoutly hoped this constable wouldn't recognise her as the guest he had spoken to earlier about finding the body.

"I finished cleaning it at about ten o'clock this morning and it was tidy when I went in there," said Lucy. "He was a very neat guest. I thought he was probably used to looking after himself."

"That's very interesting. Was that your impression too, Miss Trent?"

"Oh yes," said Irene drearily. She exchanged a look with Lucy. "I'd better tell you. I already knew him. Lucy knows. I'd rather she was here."

Inspector Maynard bent a look of approval on her. "Well now, that's a very sensible attitude, miss. How did it come about that you were acquainted with him?"

Lucy listened as Irene told the story once again. Inspector Maynard had an expression of attentiveness on his face. "He didn't tell you what his interest in the hotel was?"

"No. Just gave me my orders and expected them carried out."

"He didn't ask you about any of the guests?"

"Only who was in the room at the far corner. I told him it was the 'Society Snippets' woman and that I didn't service that room. He wanted to know who was on the top floor, but the only one I knew apart from the Carters was Mrs Portman."

"The times he called you in, did you notice anything prominent or untoward in his room?"

Irene shook her head. "No, it was like Lucy said. Tidy, apart from the first morning when the bed was a right mess."

"And how did the room look when you searched for your debt ticket?"

"The same. Tidy. Clothes hung up. Shoes in a line."

"How about his bathroom?"

"Normal."

Lucy cleared her throat. "All his toiletries were good quality. A bottle of cologne next to the mirror, expensive soap. Silver-backed brushes. Proper hair oil." She frowned. "I don't think he started out in life well-off though."

Inspector Maynard looked up alertly. "What gave you that impression?"

"I've only just thought of it. Everything about him said money, he moved as if he took having power for granted, but he didn't put his shoes out at night to be polished."

Irene nodded, agreeing with her. "That's right, you can always tell. Like he'd never got used to the idea they might not be borrowed overnight. Mind you, if he'd been staying at the Commercial, they probably would have been." She met Lucy's eyes. "Tell you what. He did ooze power, but he moved like a fighter. Very light on his feet, always aware of everything around him. And the way he talked... I reckon he'd worked his way up."

Inspector Maynard took Irene through her story again, checking the dates and who her original lender had been, then let them go. "Constable Williams will put your statements into longhand and ask you to read it through and sign it in the morning. Fetch the maitre d' along next, Williams. We'll see if he can remember who Hilliard sat with at mealtimes. If he says it's inconvenient due to being in charge of the dining room, tell him it's a good deal more inconvenient for Mr Hilliard."

Glancing at the unhappy young policeman, Lucy thought there was about as much chance of him saying that as there was of the boot boy cheeking Mr Delaney. He was only a provincial constable after all. It was a bit unfair of Inspector Maynard to tease him.

PC Williams ushered them out. "Miss Trent," he said in an awkward voice with a quick glance at the closed door. "I just wanted to say the story won't go any further. No one on the staff will hear. You won't lose your job over it."

Irene awarded him a long look. "Thanks, Billy."

The young policeman was now scarlet, as if he was forcing the words though a straight-jacket of embarrassment. "Elsie said you brought your little girl into the shop the other day. If you ever want to take her out somewhere and don't mind a bit of company, I do get some time off duty."

A trace of amusement crossed Irene's face. "Well, blow me down. How many years have you been working up to that?"

"Aw, Irene…"

To Lucy's astonishment, Irene patted his hand. "Thank you for making a rotten week better. It's my half-day on Monday if you can wangle it. Off you go and brave the dining room. Lucy and I need our beauty sleep."

She was still smiling when they reached their rooms. "Known him a while, then?" said Lucy.

"All my life," said Irene. "Billy's what you might call a slow starter. It's a pity I'm about a hundred years too old for him."

Lucy opened her door and looked back at her friend. "*He* doesn't know that. See you in the morning."

"That," said Charles to Jack. "Was not the most comfortable hour I have ever spent. Remind me to politely decline any further invitation by your uncle to conceal myself behind a firescreen in order to determine whether one Russian waiter is directing the answers of another Russian waiter under cover of translating for him."

Jack swung around from the table in their room to look at his friend. "Grigory is rather more than simply a waiter, I feel."

"Oh, I agree. The rank and file were barely breathing without checking with him whether it was permitted. One can understand why. If I'd just escaped from Bolshevik Russia, I'd be wary of authority too."

His attention sharpened. "You think they've escaped? Illegally?"

Charles's facetious air fell away. "I'd say it was borderline legal. But it's cost them. How much, I have yet to discover."

"You are sure they are legitimate émigrés?"

"Oh yes, every one of them has a contract of employment. That is all they need to get entry stamps from the port of Immingham, which, without exception, is what they have."

"Immingham, eh? Where our friend with the pleasure craft *Krista* loads and unloads his Swedish cargo?"

"If there is another Immingham along this coast, I don't know of it."

"Would you say, Charles, that the soup is starting to clear?"

"It is on my side. I will need to visit Immingham tomorrow to check, but it looks as though I can tell my lords and masters no rules are being broken. I'm not sure it gets you or Scotland Yard any further."

"No, and if I try to get a story out of it, there is a good chance none of the other poor souls still trapped in Russia will be able to escape at all." He tapped the new set of notes he was making. "We still don't know why they called Hilliard 'the wolf'."

Charles shrugged. "He was a scavenger. He may have been after pickings."

"Last time I saw him, he was after Veronique Carter."

"And yet he didn't come down to the courts to either take part in the tournament or to cheer her on."

"Perhaps he was on his way there. He was wearing tennis clothes."

"Funny sort of route that took him over the edge of a balcony."

Jack stretched moodily. "We should probably show our faces downstairs. The good thing about this hotel having so many distractions is no one knows where you are at any one time. I daresay we've been playing whist in a shadowy corner since dinner."

"Suits me. Who won?"

"A rubber each and we called it a draw."

"What are you going to do with your half day?" asked Irene as they stopped for a break mid-morning on Thursday. She was looking a good deal more cheerful this morning. Either making a clean breast of her involvement to the police, or being newly free of debt, had done wonders for her.

Flit around as Phoebe avoiding everyone who knows me as Lucy. Try and snatch a few minutes with Jack. "I don't know yet. Go into town, I expect. Why, do you want me to drop a note in at the police station for PC Williams?"

"Cheeky. No, I wondered if you were still taking it, being as it's the ball tonight. Don't you want to see the evening dresses and the jewellery?"

"We won't get to see them anyway."

"That's all you know. I plan to be very visible during the dressing hour. Just think of all those ladies on our corridor who haven't brought maids and who want a hand with hooks and buttons."

"Got it all worked out, haven't you?" said Lucy admiringly. "I'm nipping down to have a word with Myrtle. Back in five minutes if Mrs R appears."

Myrtle's face lit up when Lucy put her head around the door. She'd never seen her looking so pretty.

"How was your lunch?" asked Lucy. "I did pop in yesterday to find out, but you weren't back."

"Lucy, Gustav asked me to marry him! Me! He says he has loved me for months. He told me he does an occasional job here which helps him and helps Uncle Faun, but it won't last for ever. He has plenty of regular work with his cargo runs. He told me all about it. He brings wood-pulp, iron and ball bearings from Sweden to here and he takes back coal. He says none of it is glamorous, but it is what industry needs, so there will always be a demand. He said if I wanted to we could have a little house in Kingsthorpe as well as his home in Lysekil, then we could move between places. There's a new estate going to be built on the edge of town. Quite a lot of the Russians are interested in moving out of the staff block. I'm not surprised, it must be quite crowded. Anyway, Gustav said I couldn't work for Uncle Faun all my life and wouldn't I like a nice house and a nice husband and a nice family instead?"

"Myrtle, how wonderful! What did you say?"

"Yes," said Myrtle simply. "He is going to talk to Uncle Faun when all the unpleasantness has settled down."

Only Myrtle could describe a guest plummeting from a height and being dashed to death outside the hotel as unpleasant. "Isn't it awful?" said Lucy. "The police spoke to Irene and me yesterday evening because he was in one of the rooms on our floor. The waiters are saying he fell from a balcony."

"Uncle Faun is in a fearful stew about it. He wants notices made up for every room about using the balconies at guests' own risk. I'm typing them now."

Lucy crossed her fingers behind her back. "That's very sensible. Mr Delaney must be feeling terrible as he knew Mr Hilliard already."

"Yes, I didn't recognise his name when he booked, but I knew his face as soon as I saw him. He used to come to see Uncle Faun quite a lot when we were in Kentish Town. It was just business though. I mean, Uncle never invited him to dinner or anything."

Really, thought Lucy, it was disgracefully easy to pump Myrtle. She shouldn't be allowed out alone. "Business," she said in a dismissive voice. "That's different from being friends. I suppose it stopped when you moved up here. Even so, they must have been pleased to see each other again."

"I don't think Uncle Faun was. He never mentioned him after we moved, and he was ever so cross when Mr Hilliard came behind the counter without being asked and walked into his office."

That was a new piece of information. "What a cheek. When was that?"

"The day he got here. Uncle Faun came in and grumbled about it to me. Lucy, will you be a bridesmaid?"

"That's so sweet, but I might not still be in Kingsthorpe. Sooner or later my mother is going to need me at home again. Families are like that. You can't tell me Mr Karlsson hasn't got a handful of nieces just longing for a chance to be bridesmaids."

Myrtle happily enumerated all five of her fiancé's brothers' little girls. Lucy went back upstairs reflecting that her friend was going to fit into the Karlsson clan just fine.

She emerged from the side stairs as Chief Inspector Curtis was unlocking the door to room 1 so, after a quick look down the corridor, she slipped inside. "Mr Hilliard knew Mr Delaney in London," she said. "Myrtle says he came to their hotel several times, but it was on business."

"Did he now?" said Curtis in satisfaction. "If Xavier had loaned him money, it will be in his books. I'll put someone on to it. Tell me about this room."

"There's nothing to tell," said Lucy. "No mess, nothing disarranged apart from Tuesday morning when Irene and I think he'd had a guest overnight. Otherwise, you'd hardly know anyone was staying here."

"Anything missing as far as you can tell?"

Lucy looked at the toiletries in the bathroom and counted the seven pairs of shoes lined up along the wall. "It all seems to be here. I didn't look in the wardrobe or in the drawers. His suitcases are under the bed. I had to move them out of the way to clean, but they felt very light."

"He kept the keys for them on his ring. Habit of caution, I daresay. I shall now confirm he was right to by going through every item, every pocket and every bag. A policemen's lot is frequently tedious."

"Poor you," said Lucy with a grin. "He also, according to Myrtle, came behind the reception counter without a by your leave and went into Mr Delaney's office. Mr Delaney was furious."

"Something else to ask Delaney. I do like a nice, meaty interview. There is one curious discovery we've made, Miss Trent said she obtained a pass key for him, but the only key on him apart from his own was a duplicate to room 19."

"That's my room."
"As I said. Curious."

CHAPTER TWELVE

Lucy ate lunch with Irene, changed out of her uniform and slipped back across to the hotel. "I can't take this much more," she called to Jack from the bathroom as she once again turned into Phoebe. "Gina was on the back stairs. I had to scuttle past her all hunched up with my head down because she knows me as Phoebe."

Jack was staring out of the window. "Why would she have been on the back stairs?"

"Who knows? Her room is next to the staircase, so perhaps she used it automatically. Maybe she was looking for Mr Ward. Didn't you say he was sweet on her?"

"According to the Lester girls, he is. She was spending a fair amount of time with him and the rest of their party last night. I haven't eaten yet. Can you manage a scrap more lunch?"

"I can toy with a small helping of crab if you need company," said Lucy, emerging with her blonde wig on and an audaciously wide-brimmed pink straw hat perched at a fashionable angle.

"It's more the uncomplicated conversation I'm craving. Charles has disappeared to Immingham and I've been double-talking with the bridge set all morning. Word is the consortium is investing extensively in Kingsthorpe."

"Yes, Karlsson told Myrtle there are plans for a new estate. He's going to buy one of the small houses. Some of the Russians are interested too so I think your uncle's fears of a new gang settling in London are groundless. What's the plan for this afternoon? Who does your uncle want us to cultivate? He was brooding over Mr Hilliard's clothing when I left him earlier."

"He hasn't mentioned anyone specifically. We'll see who is downstairs and play along as the fancy takes us."

"I might quietly ask Gina if she is feeling better. I'm sure there was something else worrying her the other night. I'd still like to know why she was trying my room that first morning, and where she got the pass key. Not if Mr Oaks is hovering around her though. He won't let her say a word."

Jack frowned thoughtfully. "I haven't seen him so far today. I'll enquire of Theo and Hubert if he's staying at the Resplendent. Have you discovered why he isn't at the Bay Sands?"

"No room, I assume. Talking of which, I wonder how Lord Elvedon's aunts are coping with their nephew cluttering up their nice suite. Myrtle let slip that Mr Carter *is* paying for it, so you were right about the whole set-up being a deep-laid plan to entice the earl to Kingsthorpe."

"I thought the piling up of coincidence had his serpentine signature all over it. How did you find out?"

"Didn't I say? Gustav Karlsson has proposed. Myrtle is so dreamy she's lost any sense of discretion. She also confirmed Mr Hilliard visited Mr Delaney several times in Kentish Town on business, but that Delaney didn't like him, and also that Hilliard was confident enough to come behind the counter here and go into his office unannounced. I've told your uncle. I've also just remembered Myrtle's mother saying she was sure Mr Delaney had money troubles back in London."

"The sort of money troubles that might come from being in debt to Xavier Hilliard?"

"It would explain why he wasn't overjoyed to see him."

Jack's brow creased. "He must have paid him back though. Hilliard isn't the sort of chap you do a runner from."

"Especially if you don't change your name and you bring your widowed sister's family with you."

"Something else to think about. It may well be in his office ledgers when the Yard team get around to them. To answer your earlier question, Rupert's aunts have been playing bridge all morning. I assume they are sticking it out until he is induced to offer for Veronique. Judging by the amount of flattery being thrown in his direction last night it might not be too long. By any normal human standards, it's a terrible match for both of them. On a commercial and dynastic level, it's hard to see how either could do better."

Normal standards. Did he mean love? Was that his definition of normal? "In that case, Phoebe had better have her camera at the ready at the ball," she said lightly.

"She does have a certain facility for being in the right place at the right time when it comes to engagement announcements."

"That reminds me. I'd better tell Mrs Lester the *Chronicle* is more than willing to cover the double wedding on the terms she suggested. My editor nearly had me taking down the contract word for word over the phone. I expect they've already posted it."

"Check at the desk. I was thinking I might dally with you a bit more today. It would be natural after being thrown together by the finding of the body."

Dallying would be nice. "Careful of your reputation."

"There are times when I could cheerfully consign my reputation to the devil."

"If you do that, you'll find it harder to gather the material for your serious articles."

He took her face between his hands. "And that is one of the horns of my dilemma." He kissed her swiftly. "Lunch, before I do something shockingly out of character. There's nothing like a plate of English beef and potatoes for restoring a man to his duty."

Lucy refixed her hat and followed him. *One of the horns. What was the other? Her?*

Mr Delaney smiled with professional warmth into Mrs Portman's languorous eyes, profoundly grateful for the thirty inches of solid burr-walnut that separated her from him.

"A massage, madam?" he repeated. "Yes, I'm sure that can be arranged. As I daresay you recall, we have a suite attached to our beauty salon where Anton and his assistant Elaine ply their craft."

"Anton," murmured Mrs Portman. "It was Rudi the last time I was here. A most refreshing technique, as I recall."

"Yes indeed, but he left due to family commitments." *Due in no small part due to that technique.* "I assure you Anton is very experienced."

"Can he fit me in today? My spine feels as if it is tied up in knots. It would be a terrible shame if I had to miss the grand ball."

Behind her, Delaney saw one of the detectives cross the foyer with two suitcases that he recognised as belonging to Xavier Hilliard. Did that mean they were clearing out room 1? He returned his attention to his pampered guest and ran his finger down the appointments page. "Anton is free in half an hour, madam. Perhaps you would like to go along to the beauty salon and wait?"

"Certainly." She looked around in a leisurely fashion as if the massage suite would suddenly materialise before her.

Delaney snapped his fingers for a bell boy to show her the way.

"Delicious," she commented, her gaze resting on the youth's shining blond head and innocent blue eyes. "I'm afraid I'll have to lean on your arm."

Delaney salved his conscience by telling himself the lad had to grow up some time and reflecting that she would tip him well for the pleasure of presenting her décolletage at his eye level for the length of the passage to the beauty salon.

"That is the lady in suite 38, I believe?" said a voice at his elbow.

Delaney gave a start, instantly controlled, cursing inwardly that he hadn't noticed Chief Inspector Curtis approach the reception counter. This affair was affecting his efficiency. "Yes. Mrs Portman. She requires an emergency massage. If you will excuse me for a moment, I'll ring through so they know to expect her." He dialled the massage room extension and conversed hurriedly with Anton. The masseur replied with a Gallic snort that assured Delaney he knew exactly what sort of client Mrs Portman was.

Delaney returned his attention to the policemen.

"I wondered," said Curtis, "if Mrs Portman was on good terms with Mr Hilliard? The lift attendant recalls them entering the lift together and getting out at the top floor."

"She is a valued visitor who is on good terms with a number of the guests," he said urbanely. *Not to mention the male staff.*

"You don't know whether Hilliard had ever been invited to her suite?"

Delaney tried to look helpful. "I believe he did express

an interest in seeing the layout of the roof-terrace rooms in case he was ever in a position to book one himself."

"How kind of Mrs Portman to offer to show him hers."

"A very generous lady," confirmed Delaney.

Curtis nodded amiably and strolled away. Delaney mopped his brow with his silk handkerchief.

"And why," said Edward Carter, pausing on his way from the dining room to the gentlemen's smoking lounge, "did you not mention this fact to me?"

Because you had instructed me that you were not to be interrupted. "I hardly thought it would interest you."

"Everything that happens on the top floor interests me. When did our late, unlamented friend visit Mrs Portman?"

"I believe it was the morning after their arrival. He wasn't there long, because Mrs Portman was down to play bridge before lunch. With respect, if you are worried, she would have kept him far too busy to snoop around."

Mr Carter raised his brows. "Do you think so? If he was as good as my sources have led me to understand, she would have been pleasantly sleepy."

Mr Delaney doubted that very much, especially at mid-morning, but as it didn't do to argue with Mr Carter and he had no wish to introduce personal experience into the conversation, he simply bowed his head. "You will be kept fully informed in the future, sir."

Lucy paused at the reception counter and asked Mr Delaney's assistant if any letters had arrived for her. She was glad the manager himself was engaged with Mr Carter. The less contact she had with him the better.

"Two letters, madam," said young Quentin, sliding them across to her.

Two? Who else would be writing to Phoebe here? Lucy

smiled in thanks, being careful to keep her eyes in shadow under the brim of her hat, and put the envelopes in her handbag.

"Three for you, Mr Sinclair," said the receptionist helpfully.

Jack glanced at his envelopes with a jaundiced eye. "It'll be the family, suggesting I stop frittering away my time and put in an appearance at a wedding or a charity ball instead."

"Tiresome for you," murmured Lucy.

Jack put the letters in his jacket pocket. "I shall fortify myself with food before reading them. Where shall we sit? Hello, there are Rupert and Veronique, deep in talk. It would be indelicate to join them and waste all Veronique's hard work."

The waiter evidently thought so too. He showed them to a small separate table.

"Bribed by Carter to leave them alone?" speculated Jack.

"It's more likely that the staff want to get the large tables cleared ready for tonight," replied Lucy.

"How very prosaic." He smiled suddenly and charmingly, and devoted himself to entertaining her in his best Jack Sinclair manner.

She knew perfectly well it was largely for the benefit of the noisy party at the next table, but it was easy to relax and be diverted by his absurdity for the remainder of the meal.

"That's better," he said as they made their way to the Palm Court lounge. "You were looking altogether too self-conscious."

"How long can you keep that up for?"

"The chatter? Hours. It's verbal camouflage. The more nonsense you talk, the less people realise how clever you are. Terribly handy with the masters at school."

"And later, flitting along enemy lines?"

"Especially then. Sit down and read your letters while I get us some coffee. I can tell you want to."

The first letter was, as Lucy had expected, the document of agreement for Mrs Lester. The second was rather different. For one thing, it had been written on hotel notepaper, For another, it was printed in block capitals. And for a third...

"Tell me," she said to Jack when he returned. "Do I look particularly gullible to you?"

"Not in the remotest degree."

"And yet someone thinks I am so desperate for a scoop that I'll meet them in the tennis pavilion when everyone else is at dinner tonight."

"You're not to go."

"Of course I'm not going. I do not share your passion for putting myself in danger. Would your uncle like this letter? I've only held it by the very edges."

"Definitely, though I'm blowed if I can see a connection with the case."

"No, but he is Curtis of the Yard and we aren't."

"True. We can pass it across next time he puts in an appearance. Shall we take our coffee and join the Lester party? I shall draw the young ones' fire while you go into a respectable huddle with their mama."

"A good plan." Lucy gathered up her bag, outwardly composed. "All the same, my room's had an intruder, Gina was trying my door with a pass key, and now this. Why me? I don't like it."

"No more do I. If Uncle Bob can't work it out, we'll have to. I may invite you to stroll with me along the beach this afternoon in order to cogitate." He raised his voice as he dropped into a chair next to Amanda Lester. "My spies tell me you have been devising a new dance step. Are we to have the pleasure of seeing it at the ball tonight?"

Mrs Lester looked up, tolerantly amused. Lucy realised with some surprise that she'd been talking amicably to Gina Bianca and Jimmy Ward. You'd never have thought she'd looked at Gina so coldly that first night.

"I certainly hope so, the amount they have been practising," she said. She noticed Lucy hovering and at once her smile became a trifle frozen. "Do sit down, Miss Sugar. I've been monopolising Miss Bianca quite enough."

"Thank you." Lucy gave Gina a sideways, comradely smile. It was clear the actress was far more relaxed than at any point so far this week. "No Mr Oaks?" she murmured.

"We had words yesterday. He's pushed off. He won't stay away though, worse luck."

Jimmy immediately said, "I keep telling you, Gina, if you'd only..." The rest of his sentence was lost as he lowered his voice.

Lucy turned to Mrs Lester, half-extracting the contract out of her bag. "I don't know if this is a convenient moment to ...?" Out of the corner of her eye, she saw Gina briefly press Jimmy's hand.

Mrs Lester glanced at the envelope with something very like distaste. "Thank you. May I take it and read it through?"

"Of course. There is no hurry at all." *Which wasn't quite what her editor had said, but she was here and her editor wasn't.*

"I have been wondering if I was a little too hasty... but I suppose it might be as well." She gazed into the distance for a moment, then briskly tucked the contract into her bag. "Thank you. I'll let you know. Now then, what are you young people going to do this afternoon? The golf club has a croquet lawn if you are interested."

"Nobody plays croquet any more, Mummy," said Amanda.

"We thought we'd swim, didn't we, Theo," said Julie.

"Be sure to back in time to bathe and change." She stood. "I have an appointment at the beauty salon. I will see you all later."

"Do you want to swim, Gina?" said Jimmy.

She turned large blue eyes on him, still holding his hand. "Won't it be cold?"

"Bracing," said Hubert.

Jimmy ignored him. "We could play billiards instead if you would prefer that."

"I would," she replied thankfully. "I'm not very good though."

"I'll coach you."

"Would you? Thank you. I always feel safe in your hands."

And if that wasn't a 'come hither' line, Lucy had never heard one. Gina really was a different woman when Oaks wasn't around.

"What are you going to do, Phoebe?" asked Amanda.

"I wouldn't mind a walk on the beach, but I didn't bring a costume. I'm happy to photograph those of you who did."

The twins got up in a giggling rush. "We'll see you down there. The boys can use Jimmy's room to change and spare our blushes. You don't mind, do you, Jimmy?"

He looked away from Gina, slightly dazzled. "Feel free. Tell the bod behind the counter I said you could borrow my key. The spares are all on a board. Handy when you've left yours in the wrong pocket."

"I swam earlier," said Jack. He turned to Lucy. "May I have the pleasure of escorting you to the bay?"

Julie made a mock-dramatic gesture. "Oh, are you falling for Jack, Phoebe? Don't do it. He'll break your heart."

"He broke mine," said Amanda mournfully. They each bestowed a butterfly kiss on him and departed upstairs to change.

Jimmy piloted Gina towards the billiard room.

"His devotion is doing wonders for her self-esteem," commented Jack.

"He's been in love with her for a couple of years," said Hubert. "Can't think why they haven't tied the knot yet."

"By the looks of things today, he might be about to get his wish. Another nice splash for your paper, Phoebe."

As he spoke, Jack's fingers brushed Lucy's shoulder. She followed his gaze and saw the Scotland Yard detectives crossing the reception hall towards the small sitting room. She stood up. "I'll see you outside," she said, and headed in Mr Curtis's direction.

"Left at the desk, you say?" Jack's uncle lifted the single sheet of Bay Sands Hotel notepaper with tweezers to inspect both sides. "Have you got the envelope? I'll give them to Draper, but I doubt he'll get any useful prints. Criminals are too clever nowadays. I blame all these detective stories."

Lucy, who wrote those self-same stories, grinned at him. "Can't solve a mystery these days without them. Sorry."

Jack sidled into the room. "The paper and envelopes are available in all the sitting rooms. It could have been written by anyone, then slid on to the desk in passing."

Maynard stood up. "I'll ask the masterpiece on the counter if anyone remembers when it appeared." He padded out.

"Meanwhile," said Curtis. "What do you know about Mrs Thalia Portman?"

"Wealthy widow, several times over," said Jack. "Exhibitionist. Man hungry. Approach with extreme caution."

"Here in search of the next husband?"

"I wouldn't think so, no. Thalia prefers the lower orders. Chauffeurs, croupiers, bartenders, dancing professionals etc. I am told by those shaken by the experience that she has no problem with privacy. Beaches, lonely country roads and woodland appear to especially amuse her. If she has to make do with an indoor venue, leaving all the doors and windows open adds to the spice."

"That's true," confirmed Lucy. "The upstairs chambermaids say they've had to close the door to her suite themselves. There have been complaints from the people on either side of her terrace about her french windows being left open and I saw for myself that she doesn't bother drawing the blinds."

"If she is that uninhibited, I'm surprised she hasn't made use of the terrace itself," said Maynard, returning. "Nobody saw your letter arrive. The young assistant noticed it around lunchtime on Wednesday and put it in your pigeonhole."

"That doesn't surprise me," said Lucy. "The reception hall gets very busy before and after meals. As for Mrs Portman, Mr Delaney asked her not to use the terrace. Myrtle says there were words about it the last time she stayed. Even so, she was apparently out there with a very amorous chap just after breakfast one morning. The ladies in 37 were incensed, that not being at all the sort of thing they are used to. I don't know who the man was. They thought he looked like a waiter, according to the chambermaids."

"She does seem to be making a tally of them," said Jack.

Curtis drummed his fingers. "She prefers to sport with the staff, and yet she spent time with Xavier Hilliard. It could have been him the ladies saw. Make a note to ask them, Maynard. Did she sense a touch of the gigolo, perhaps?"

Lucy put her head on one side. "Possibly. I thought when he was dancing with Gina Bianca, before Jack told me who he was, that he looked like a lounge lizard. There was something continental in the way he moved."

Jack nodded. "That's it. You've put your finger on it."

Curtis exchanged a glance with Maynard. "Our people are looking into his history. Might be worth asking them to look a little faster. Meanwhile, I think it's time we had another chat with our Mr Delaney."

Lucy stood up hastily. "Just let me get out of the way first."

As fast as she was, Jack was before her to open the door. "To the beach," he said. "See if we can remember how ordinary people enjoy themselves."

CHAPTER THIRTEEN

Delaney assumed a helpful expression as Inspector Maynard approached the reception counter. He supposed it was too much to ask that they had finished their investigations and were preparing to leave the hotel.

The policeman smiled affably back at him. "Mr Curtis wonders if you wouldn't mind popping into the sitting room for a few minutes," he said. "One or two questions have arisen."

Delaney's hopes faded. What sort of questions, he wondered. "Certainly. Take over," he said to his assistant, and walked across the intervening space with his usual serene air.

Curtis was seated at the larger of the writing desks. "Sit down, Mr Delaney. I've had a man looking into Hilliard's business affairs in London. Why did you not mention you were already on terms of intimacy with him?"

Delaney recoiled. "Hardly intimacy." *So much for Xavier destroying the original paperwork.*

"Enough for him to come into your office without an invitation, I'm told. Yet you gave the impression that he was simply a guest."

"He was. Ours was a financial arrangement which terminated some time ago. He came to the office to ask about swapping his room."

"Indeed? I saw no fault with his room. Why would he wish to change?"

Delaney's mind went blank. "He... he wondered if there was one with a view of the golf course."

"I see." Curtis made a note. "You borrowed money from him to keep your previous hotel afloat, I believe."

Delaney gave a practised smile. "Purely a temporary loan to tide me over a period when various financial obligations all accrued at once."

"Infuriating when that happens," murmured Curtis. "The trouble with temporary loans is that they have a habit of becoming permanent the more the interest builds up."

Don't they just. Especially with a devious, twisting bastard like Xavier holding the hotel deeds. "This *was* temporary, Chief Inspector. The loan was paid off. Mr Hilliard booked his stay here in the conventional manner."

"So you didn't see him when he made a visit to Kingsthorpe a few months ago?"

"No," he said, perturbed. *Hilliard had been up before? Sneaking around while the hotel was being built or fitted out? Why?*

"Did he make any specific requests about his accommodation when he booked?"

How did he know all of this? "My niece deals with that side of things. She sees to the bookkeeping and the reservations."

The detective made another note. "I see. Tell me, how did you pay off the debt to Mr Hilliard?"

Delaney felt his pulse rate leap. "As it happened, I received an offer for my hotel. It was sufficient to pay off the loan and move here to Kingsthorpe with my sister and her family." *And if I had known how badly Xavier Hilliard would have taken being paid back in full, I would have been much more discreet about my plans. I ought to have simply paid him, got the deeds back and left it at that.*

146

"But you do not own the Bay Sands Hotel?"

"No, I am a paid employee. Far less of a strain on the wallet." He trotted the joke out automatically.

"I can see the attraction. Though I daresay the profit margins on a resort hotel are rather different to those of a pied a terre for commercial travellers in Kentish Town. I understand the site is now occupied by a cigarette factory, is that right? One belonging to Mr Edward Carter."

"That is not my concern. Nowadays I concentrate wholly on delivering an enjoyable experience to my guests."

"Like Mrs Portman, for instance. When did she make her booking?"

Delaney could feel himself breaking out into a light sweat. Why all these questions when the police were supposed to be looking into Xavier Hilliard's death? "I am afraid I don't know. As I said, my niece deals with the reservations. Mrs Portman stayed with us earlier in the year. She may have made a repeat booking then. Many regular guests do so, in order not to be disappointed later if their choice of room is taken."

"Perhaps I may venture into your niece's fastness and check up with her? Miss Myrtle Smith, is that right?"

Delaney looked at him in dismay. "Yes, but ..." He stopped. "If I might ask, what has Mrs Portman's reservation to do with Mr Hilliard's unfortunate accident?" he said.

"It's simply routine. Ninety percent of our job entails asking routine questions which are then discarded as irrelevant. Isn't that so, Maynard?"

"Indeed it is," said the other detective.

Delaney rose, not believing either of them. "I will see if Myrtle is free."

The Bay Sands Hotel provided deckchairs and rugs for those guests who wished to enjoy the curving expanse of sand without the risk of spoiling their beach outfits. For once, Jack wasn't thinking about work or life or the future. He was simply sitting on a rug next to Lucy, watching Gustav Karlsson's yacht tack back and forth across the bay. "This is nicer than writing letters to each other," he said. "Do you realise we only had that one week together in London before you were torn away from me to come up here?"

She gave a rueful smile. "Not long enough, was it? It's your own fault for not looking where you were going in New York, then introducing me to your uncle as soon as you found me again."

"I didn't expect him to be quite so quick off the mark." He broke off as Charles lowered himself elegantly down beside them. "Go away, Charles, I'm dallying."

"Not in broad daylight, old man, not at all the thing. Wouldn't you like to hear the fruits of my labours, vis-à-vis our Russian friends?"

Jack gave a resigned sigh. "I knew this was too good to be true. We'll dally another time, Lucy. What have you found out?"

"And how?" asked Lucy.

"Charles has even more mysterious ways than I do. He probably knows how their passages are arranged, who brings them over and what the payment is on their part."

"Not quite," replied Charles modestly. "By judicious listening-in, I believe the Russian fixer to be Grigory's brother-in-law. The mode of transport for the last leg is by sea from Sweden in one of Karlsson's cargo steamers. The émigrés are then, I suggest, ferried down the coast in a certain gaff cutter."

"Hence why his presence is required at the consortium's meetings up here."

"I imagine so. The reason I have been absent all morning is because I have been in Immingham, interviewing a member of the border force who makes sporadic trips out to cargo ships moored in the harbour, inspects and stamps the papers of displaced persons wishing to make an honest living in Britain and is returned to shore again, having been adequately recompensed for his out-of-hours services."

"Good heavens. Did he know he was talking to you?"

"Give me credit for some sense, Jack. I was a gentleman ship owner wondering if I might make some such arrangement of the sort myself."

"And how did you find out about Grigory's brother-in-law?" asked Lucy. "Not that I'm doubting you. It makes perfect sense that Grigory is involved."

"I fetched my sketching apparatus and sat outside the open kitchen door."

"So simple when you know how," murmured Jack.

"But none of the Russian staff are prosperous," said Lucy. "How would they have paid their passage?"

"Perhaps that's the reason they are not prosperous," said Charles.

Jack shook his head. "Somebody must be. It takes money to arrange travel papers, passports and rail tickets. It's difficult to see Grigory's brother-in-law doing it out of the goodness of his heart. Equally, it's difficult to see Edward Carter bankrolling the operation simply to get cheap staff for his hotel. We're missing something obvious."

Lucy looked towards the hotel where Gina was picking her way down the steps, heading for a pair of deckchairs with a canopy above them. "So is Gina. No Mr Oaks and no Mr Ward. I will see if I can have a girlish chat with her."

She got up and strolled in her direction. Jack felt a touch bereft.

Gina peered at Lucy over the top of her dark glasses. "I decided to join you after all. Mr Lester asked Jimmy to go through a report for him."

"Businessmen never stop working, do they?" said Lucy. "When are your publicity photos being done?"

Gina looked alarmed. "Which photos?"

Too late, Lucy remembered it was Myrtle who had told her about the publicity shots when she was allocating the bedrooms. As Phoebe, she oughtn't to know anything about it. "Oh," she said vaguely. "I thought I overheard the manager saying something about how you would be using the bay as a backdrop from your balcony."

"Oh that. No, I cancelled them. I'm in the wrong room. It was supposed to be the other corner. My room looks back along towards the town. I wanted the empty road and the open sea."

"Maddening," said Lucy. "I'd offer you the use of my balcony, but the police say I have to keep off it. I can take one of you on the jetty, if you like. Leaning on the rail looking delighted with life, with the sea sparkling away in the background. If it's not what you want, you don't have to use it."

Gina turned and looked judiciously at the jetty. "I don't mind trying. It would be nice to have an exterior shot. I'm not really an outdoors person. The film studio tears you off a strip if you get too much colour from the sun."

"That's a shame. You miss out on quite a lot of fun. The beach and tennis and golf are part of the attraction of staying in a resort hotel."

"I suppose so. I've only been to Cannes and a place on the south coast before. I'm told where to be seen. Ronnie was furious about me coming here when it hadn't been arranged by the studio. That's partly why he's been in such a foul temper."

"But you stood up for yourself. Well done."

Just for a moment Gina looked frightened. As if she'd been caught out. "Oh, well, there was a whole crowd coming. I was wondering..."

Lucy was visited by the oddest notion. Had the actress been *told* to come up here? Evidently not by Mr Oaks. By Hilliard? She remembered again that she'd had a pass key and Hilliard, crucially, hadn't. "Yes?"

"When will it be in the paper? About Xavier... about the accident?"

Now, why would that matter? "I phoned through the story yesterday that there had been a fatal accident. I haven't seen the *Chronicle* today."

"Did you name him?" Gina's voice was sharp.

"The police asked me not to. Besides, I do fashion and women's pages, not the sensational stuff."

"That's nicer." Gina spoke absently, her face reflecting inner calculation.

Lucy was reminded of what Charles had said about Mrs Lester's expression. "When are you due back on set?" she asked.

"Next week. I'll be glad. It's a lot easier, filming. The director tells me what to do and I do it."

Jimmy Ward was coming out of the hotel entrance and heading for the beach. Lucy wouldn't have much more time to fish for information. "Did you know Mr Hilliard well?" she asked.

Gina seemed unsurprised at the question. "Clever, aren't you? I've known Xavier a long time, for my sins. How could you tell?"

"I thought when you were dancing with him that it didn't look as if he was a stranger."

151

"You're observant too. People like us are, aren't we? I hardly ever see him these days, but it's always the same when I do. I'm under his spell, just like I always was. I made a picture once where the heroine is hypnotised by a swaying snake. That was Xavier. Even when I was involved with him, I hated him. He wasn't a nice person. I'm glad he's dead."

"Gina!" There was a shout from the terrace.

Gina turned, her face transformed. "Jimmy, just in time. Phoebe is going to take a photo of me on the jetty. Do you want to watch?"

"Careful you don't fall in."

"I won't if you are there to take care of me. I always feel safe with you."

Lucy got to her feet. Gina appeared to be making the most of Mr Oaks's absence to form a rather healthier relationship. She'd take a couple of photographs of the actress and then she'd relay the latest information to Jack.

"I believe Gina was told to book her room by Hilliard. She's known him for a long time, refers to him as Xavier and I *think* he must have had a hold over her. She'd never been to Kingsthorpe before, but knew to ask for a corner room and the reason to give. But because Myrtle thinks of 1, 25 and 37 as being corner rooms, it was the wrong end of the hotel. I'm sure Hilliard was the person who gave her the staff key. Goodness knows what she was supposed to be doing in my room."

"Didn't you ask her?"

"I didn't even ask if she'd been ordered to book. We aren't quite at that level of intimacy yet."

"Well then, can you find out how much she knows of Hilliard's past?"

"I can try."

Jack swung around to look pensively at the hotel. "There is a man on your balcony," he observed.

"Again?" said Lucy.

"Two men," said Charles.

"Fenn and Draper, looking for prints," said Jack. "I'd have thought they'd have checked at first light."

"Good luck to them. We don't clean the balconies as rigorously as we do the insides of the rooms. The rail will be a mass of prints. I hope they finish before I have to change for dinner."

"Plenty of time until then."

Lucy shook her head. "I need to be ready early so Irene doesn't come knocking on the door asking if I need help fastening my dress. Phoebe ought to be on hand to record the glamorous outfits anyway. I'd better lock this film away and put a new one in. If we've got time, I'll go into Kingsthorpe and get them developed so I can send some prints to the *Chronicle*."

Jack was still looking at the hotel. "It might have to be tomorrow. I rather fancy we are being waved at. There are now three men on your balcony and one of them is Uncle Bob."

"Cause of death was by falling on to a hard surface from a considerable height, and would have been instantaneous. Balcony rails are an orgy of prints. Eliminating all the irrelevant ones is going to take a while. Some are quite clear though. Hilliard's have been found on the rooftop rail *underneath* those belonging to Mr and Miss Carter."

Jack nodded. "Meaning it was him I saw on Tuesday outside Carter's suite, since when the rightful occupants have leant on the rail."

"That's how we read it."

"But he didn't fall from there on Wednesday?"

"It's not ruled out. He could have toppled over - or been thrown over - without touching it."

"He didn't give the impression of a man who would do anything of the sort without putting up a strenuous defence," said Jack drily.

"I agree. The pathologist didn't find evidence of the sort of bruising that would arise from a fight." Curtis shot them both a considering glance. "Draper has found Hilliard's prints on Lucy's balcony rail."

Apprehension ran through Lucy, though she'd known all along, really. "On mine?"

"Yes, quite a number of them. I'm going to have to ask you to stay off the balcony. Normally I'd ask the guest to move rooms, but I think we can trust you."

"Added to which, the only free room is Hilliard's own," murmured Jack.

"What about his shoes?" asked Lucy. "Did you discover what he had been walking in?"

Curtis looked startled. "I beg your pardon?"

"His shoes. The white tennis shoes with the thin crepe soles. They were clean in the morning, and were smeared with something white when we... when we found him. I wondered if he'd slipped."

Curtis fished a sheet of paper out of the folder he was carrying. "His shoes are not mentioned in the report. Where are Fenn's photos?" He riffled through them. "Hilliard's shoes were clean."

Lucy sat up straight. "I'm sorry, but they weren't. I took a photograph myself."

"What an intelligent young woman you are. Do you have the film?"

"Yes, but I haven't had it developed."

"I'll get your rolls," said Jack, leaving the room.

"Something white. Powder, perhaps?" Curtis stared into space. Lucy had the impression he was thinking furiously.

The door opened and Jack came back in with a handful of film canisters. "I brought them all," he said apologetically. "Didn't know which was which."

"That was quick, thank you," said Curtis. "Fenn can develop them. He has commandeered a darkroom in Kingsthorpe. He and Draper are checking the second floor balconies at the moment."

Lucy turned to Jack. "Someone cleaned Hilliard's shoes? When?"

"At a guess, when they were covering him up in full view of us," said Jack in a disgusted voice. "We resign, Uncle Bob. We are demonstrably unfit for active service."

"Why would they clean them?" said Lucy.

Jack shrugged. "Because they are Russian and until recently were oppressed in their own land. I don't know. Ask them. It was Pyotr in charge of the tarpaulin."

Pyotr, who had been so animated talking about roof pitches and angles. Pyotr who had hurried up with the groundsheet, his face full of concern. Lucy remembered again taking the photographs, horror in the viewfinder at odds with the clean scent of lavender in the air.

"Lavender," she said suddenly.

Curtis raised his eyebrows. "I beg your pardon?"

"There are no plants at the front of the hotel."

Jack looked at her consideringly. "There aren't, no. It is all very modern. Why?"

She pointed at the tin of talcum powder on her dressing table. "Lavender," she said again.

"I know. You use it when you are being Phoebe. It smells delightful."

Curtis cleared his throat. "Time and a place, nephew."

She met Jack's eyes. "But I wasn't wearing it when we found Hilliard, because I was late and had scrambled to get

155

changed. Jack, I smelt lavender when I was photographing him." She shuddered violently. "I thought the tin felt lighter than it should have done when I used it earlier."

"You think someone had dusted his shoes with talcum powder?" said Jack. "That's ridiculous. He would have noticed. He'd have slid all over the place."

Curtis frowned. "Talcum powder. Would it smell strong enough?"

Lucy sprang up, reaching for her jar of cold cream before remembering about fingerprints and snatching her hand back. "Maybe not, but that does. I bought it for Phoebe because it was cheap and the girl in the chemist said it was lavender-scented. She wasn't wrong. It's appalling. I only used it once. It's also unpleasantly thick and greasy. The jar should be nearly full."

Carter dropped his handkerchief over it and lifted it gingerly. "It doesn't feel it. It feels close to empty. Stay here, you two. Guard those. Write down everything else you have noticed. I'll nip upstairs to get Draper. After he's printed this jar and the tin, he can try going more thoroughly over Hilliard's shoes." He hurried out.

CHAPTER FOURTEEN

Lucy sat down abruptly on the bed. "Why this room, Jack? Why my talcum powder? Why my cream? I don't understand."

"The cosmetics, I fancy, *because* they were in this room," said Jack slowly. "As for why this room..." He glanced upwards. "Who is above you?"

"Mr and Mrs Lester."

"And above them is Mr Carter, outside whose suite on the day after my arrival I saw a furtive white-clad figure we believe to have been Xavier Hilliard listening to whatever was going on inside."

Lucy dragged her mind back. It seemed much more distant than a scant two days ago. "That was the meeting between the consortium who own the hotel and Mr Karlsson." She recalled the scene in the dining room as the men had got up from the table. "There were two or three other gentlemen as well. I didn't recognise them, but they looked like businessmen. Maybe Grigory too. Mr Carter was talking to him and pointing upwards."

"That's the one. While it was taking place, you were kept downstairs by Mrs Lester. Mr Hilliard had a key enabling him to make use of this room. His prints have been found on the balcony. I wonder..." Jack hunted in his pocket for a pair of thin gloves.

"Why do you have cotton gloves in your pockets?"

"Habit," he said, easing his fingers into them. Then he opened the door on to the balcony.

"Your uncle said not to touch anything," Lucy reminded him.

"That's why I've got gloves on. Lucy, come out here. Do you see what I see?"

Lucy stepped out, into the shelter of his arm, and looked where he was looking. "I see the jetty. I see Mr Karlsson tying up his tender. He must have finished sailing for the day."

"Closer than that."

"I see the coast road. I see the start of the golf course."

"Closer than that."

"I see the balcony rail. I see the ornamental boss you want to stand a pot plant on. I see the corner of the building."

Jack's voice was very soft. "And?"

Lucy looked. The balcony, railed off to the front and side. The ceramic ledge with its absurd truncated column. The bare wall of the hotel, sheer from ground level to the roof terraces. The... "Oh," she said, enlightenment dawning. "The drainpipe."

Jack let out a long breath. "The drainpipe. A sturdy drainpipe, white-painted so as not to spoil the look of the facade. I'll bet if you balanced on this rail and stretched across you could get to it with the help of that ornamental ledge. And if you were very agile and very confident and had thin crepe soles on your shoes to give you a good grip, you could then climb the drainpipe all the way to the roof terraces - Hilliard's fingerprints were on the rail, remember - and eavesdrop on a business meeting with no one inside being any the wiser. I wonder if Draper tested the wall for hand prints? Hilliard would need to have steadied himself before leaping across."

"He must *really* have been confident," said Lucy, measuring it by eye. On the ground, it would be an easy leap. Up here... "Wait, didn't one of your rumours have him escaping from a circus years ago?"

"It did indeed. Can you have another chat with Gina to find out if she knows his history? If we are right, it would explain why he wanted this room."

"It doesn't explain the talcum powder or the..." Lucy's voice tailed off... "Jack, if someone suspected he was using the drainpipe, someone tall and ruthless maybe, they could also balance on the rail, then reach across and shake talcum powder on to the drainpipe. It wouldn't be seen until it was too late, until Hilliard scrabbled for a purchase which wasn't there."

Jack gave her a sombre look. "And if the breeze blew the talcum powder away, that same someone could unscrew the lid of your jar of lavender-scented cold cream and slap a fair old handful on the ornamental ledge. Even from this distance, I don't think it looks quite as pristine and smooth as it did when I made the crack about the flower pot."

Lucy looked at the absurd, decorative ledge, horror clutching at her. "And so Xavier Hilliard - intent on finding something damning in Mr Carter's suite - balances on my balcony, leaps lightly on to the boss on the way to the drainpipe and..." She bit her lips together, swallowing hard. "I feel sick."

Lucy went down alone for tea. Her room was suddenly rather more full of large detectives than she was altogether comfortable with. She had, it was true, watched the 'flash and dabs' procedures with close interest for use in future Leonora Benson detective novels, but after being asked for the third time to move out of the way, she thought it best to efface herself completely.

She paused in the reception hall to get her camera out. Framed by the Egyptian-style archway of the Palm Court lounge, Gina Bianca and Jimmy Ward made a touching picture. They were standing near the ornamental fountain, but Jimmy was obviously so radiantly happy he hadn't noticed his blazer was soaked with spray.

"There's a jeweller in the town," he was saying. "I'm going in right now to see what he has. I'm too excited for tea. Gina, you've made me so happy. We are going to *be* so happy."

He raced past Lucy and out of the hotel entrance. She put the camera back and quickly lengthened her stride to reach the actress before anyone else got there.

"Sorry, I couldn't help overhearing. Do I gather congratulations are in order? I must get a photograph of the two of you tonight. What are you going to wear?"

Gina looked at her in something very like panic. "I don't know. Help me, Phoebe. I've angled for this, and I've got it, and it was easy, and now I feel terrible."

Lucy signalled to one of the waiters. "Sit down and let's have tea. I defy anyone to be miserable with a plate of cakes inside them."

"I can't. I'm supposed to watch my weight. Oh... it doesn't matter now, does it?" She gave an uncertain laugh. "Ronnie is going to be livid. Can you keep it out of the paper?"

Lucy shook her head regretfully. "I'm sorry. I'd get the sack. You are big news with 'Society Snippets' readers. The *Chronicle* would probably make me pay my own bill if I didn't report your engagement. What's the problem?" She took her arm to guide her to one of the low tables. Gina gave a yelp and put a hand to her shoulder. Lucy looked more closely. "That's a nasty bruise. Have you put arnica on it?"

Gina shook her head, sitting down and adjusting her

cap sleeve to cover it. "No point. I bruise easily and recover easily. It'll fade. They always have before."

They both fell silent as one waiter presented them with a tiered stand of cakes and another poured tea into geometrically-patterned cups.

Gina picked hers up. "I suppose I'm panicking. I just…" She broke off. "I saw you with Jack Sinclair earlier. Have you got a woo going. You looked more than pally, if you know what I mean."

Lucy made a snap decision. Gina might open up more if she detected fellow feeling. She dropped her voice. "Yes. I didn't intend to because of being nobody in real life and he's one of the Sinclairs, but I do like him an awful lot. He knows about Phoebe being a pen name, I couldn't deceive him about that. He says he doesn't mind, but I'm worried what his friends will think when I turn up on his arm as me. They might never talk to either of us again. Even worse, what are his family going to say when they know I'm a society reporter on the side?"

"That's it, isn't it?" said Gina. "The different worlds thing. I've felt a fraud ever since I hit the big time. Will you fit into his set?"

"I don't know. I can certainly try. My father's in racing, so it might help."

Gina nibbled her way along a chocolate fancy. "It's very shallow, very artificial, very fast-paced. It's not real, but I've got used to it and I don't want to lose it. I don't want to be no one again. I couldn't bear to go back to that life. That's one reason I said yes to Jimmy."

"I don't understand. Why would you ever be no one?"

It was Gina's turn to lower her voice. "There's a new craze coming. Talking pictures. Ronnie says they are going to be huge. Don't breathe a word, but he's heard Al Jolson is recording musical numbers *right now* in America for a film. The cinematographer lines up the gramophone record with the film reel so they match before they show it. Then they play both together. Songs on the screen. Can you believe that?"

Lucy stared at her over the rim of her teacup. "It'll never work."

"It does, there have been short pictures made, but it's ghastly when it goes wrong. Ronnie says they'll iron that out. He says we'll be rich as kings. He's wrong. I can't sing, Phoebe. The film company won't want me any more. I'm terrified."

"But Gina, your speaking voice is all right. Why does not being able to sing matter?"

"That's what they'll concentrate on to begin with. That's their way in. And my speaking voice isn't all right, not really. The film company took some of us to Chelmsford last year to talk on the radio and it was awful."

She had clearly made up her mind. "Talking pictures might never happen," said Lucy, "or not for a long time."

Gina shook her head. "I'm not going to take the risk. I'm not going to hang on, hoping. Don't you see? As soon as I stop making pictures, I'll be nobody."

"Jimmy will still love you."

"I know he will. I *am* ashamed of this, Phoebe, but marrying him means I can retire from the pictures now, while I'm a success. I won't be dropped because I'm a failure." Her face set with determination. "I'm not going to cheat on him. I'm more fond of Jimmy than I am of anyone. I just want out of the business. I want to marry him and be looked after and have kiddies and give them a damn sight better life than I ever got. That's the other reason I said yes. I couldn't before, because Xavier was so unpredictable. Jimmy is tough enough to protect me from Ronnie, but he would have been no match for Xavier. Jimmy works in banking, you see. I like him too much to risk what Xavier might have asked me to do next. But now he's dead, so it's all right."

"You knew Hilliard that well?"

She gave a short laugh. "We went way back. I met Xavier when I was doing variety. The human flea, that's how they billed him. Leaps and jumps like you wouldn't believe. He had been part of a foreign acrobatic troupe when he was a kid, but they beat him, so he waited and planned and one day he poisoned their stew pot, then did a runner with the money. He did a juggling-come-tumbling act by night, went with the men after the show and blackmailed them the next day. He wasn't fussy about gender. Got his first house deeds when one of his lovers shot himself. He used that to finance his moneylending business."

The human flea. Someone who wouldn't think twice about leaping from a balcony rail to a drainpipe using a small ceramic ledge as a stepping stone. Lucy did her best to look open-mouthed. "But what does that have to do with you? I mean, I can see he'd be a force to be reckoned with, but did he have a hold on you?"

Gina looked at her candidly. "Xavier had something on everybody he ever met. It was an obsession. I had a room in the same house as him back in the old days and I had a fall and couldn't work for a while. I was having trouble with the rent so he got me a modelling job to pay off the arrears. It was really well paid which should have made me smell a rat. It turned out I was modelling myself. No clothes required. Dirty photos for dirty old men. Xavier bought the negatives. This is the first time he's ever used them. He could have ruined me."

"How awful. What did he want you to do?"

"Come up here for the opening and stay alone. Book a corner room. When it turned out to be the wrong one, he gave me a key and said to move things around in your room so you'd demand a different one and he could swap with you. But you were working in it, so I didn't." She gave

Lucy an apologetic grin. "I'm glad of that, now I know you."

"Why my room? Why did he want that end of the hotel?"

Gina ate another cake. "He didn't tell me. I was so scared of him, I couldn't disobey when he told me to do things. Ronnie was livid I was coming up here without him. I had to tell him about the dirty photos to shut him up. If Xavier had published them, they'd have finished my career and Ronnie knew it. He still didn't trust me though. He went and booked in at the Commercial to keep an eye on me. I was *so* cross with him. I told him Xavier said it was all right for him to be here during the day, but not evenings or dinner. He hadn't said anything of the sort, but I just wanted time to myself. That's why I'd originally told Jimmy I was coming up here, so we could be together quietly. God knows what Ronnie will do when he hears about us. I'm hoping it'll be something that will put him behind bars. Just as long as he doesn't hurt Jimmy. He'll probably have a go at him. It's usually fists with Ronnie. I saw enough of that when I was growing up."

Lucy ate a cake and poured out the last of the tea. Through the Egyptian archway, she saw Inspector Maynard cross the reception hall and enter the small sitting room. With a surreal feeling of deja vu, she said. "You won't like this, but I think you should tell the police about Hilliard and about Mr Oaks threatening you. Then if something does happen, you won't have to prove your story from a standing start, will you? And in case they find out anyway, it's always good to have got in first."

Like Irene before her, Gina looked aghast. "I can't do that. They'll think it gives me a motive for killing Xavier."

"Don't be silly, you were at the tennis every moment from lunch until dinner, and even with dance training, I can't believe you'd have been able to tip him over a balcony rail if he didn't want to go."

Gina nodded slowly. "You're right." She stood up, precarious resolution in every line. "I'll do it before I lose my nerve." She glanced at the empty cake stand. "Those things are dangerous."

Lucy waited in the lounge. Presumably someone would tell her when she could get back into her room to change. All around her, teapots were refreshed, cake stands replaced, the hum of conversation grew louder.

Eventually Jack sauntered in and dropped into the chair vacated by Gina. "Your room is free. Some very puzzling prints, according to Draper. He and Fenn are heading back to that darkroom they've borrowed."

"Puzzling?"

"I was told no more than that but they were giving the wall outside your room the full treatment and leaning out at full stretch to inspect the ornamental boss. May I pick up your hand and secretly play with your fingers like suitors from the olden days?"

"No. You can ask for more tea and listen to what Gina told me."

"We were right about Hilliard originally being an acrobat then. Uncle Bob needs to know this," said Jack when she had finished.

"Inspector Maynard will tell him. Here's Gina now, shaken, but unburdened."

"And here is Jimmy Ward. Love must agree with him. I've never seen him looking so alert."

Jack stood up as Gina entered. "May I offer you some tea, Miss Bianca?"

"Tea nothing, this calls for champagne," interrupted Jimmy, his face flushed and his normally vague expression completely absent.

Gina perked up. "Did you find one?"

"I'll say. I got to the jeweller just as the shop was closing. The chap on the counter had gone home, but the old guy who runs the place was still there and got out all his trays for me to look at. I chose this." He presented a small box to Gina and lifted the hinged lid.

Gina gasped. "It's so sparkly. Diamonds are my favourite. Jimmy, it's gorgeous."

He slid the ring on to her finger. "There, you can't go back on your word now. Do you really like it? Dammit, where's that waiter with the champagne?"

Gina nodded fervently, angling her hand, unable to take her eyes off the ring.

"It's lovely," put in Lucy. Mr Ward had been really very clever. A platinum setting to match Gina's hair, slim enough to fit her hand, but with a quietly emphatic presence. "Was that the new shop in town?"

Jimmy nodded and addressed himself to Gina again. "He said this one was an old, old diamond, but in a new setting. I said I thought you'd prefer that." He looked at her anxiously. "You know, having something new, just for you."

"Oh yes," said Gina. "Jimmy, it's beautiful. I love the tiny diamonds clustered around the central one, just as if they're protecting it. What's the pattern on the band? It's so pretty."

At this, Jimmy turned pink. "I wondered about that too. Karlsson came in while I was there - he's the Swedish chap who owns the yacht in the bay. He wanted to look through the rings as well. I made a comment about the engraving, and he jabbered away with the old chap in some foreign lingo, then told me the tracery is braided wheat, like when they make a harvest sheaf of bread in the church at home. Apparently ears of wheat are symbols for luck and fertility where this jeweller comes from. Karlsson gave a great shout of laughter and said he wanted wheat engraving on the ring he was buying too. Do you really like it, Gina?"

Gina was looking at him with eyes that were only slightly less starry than the brilliance of the diamond at the centre of her ring. "Jimmy, I love it. I'll wear it for ever."

His voice dropped. "And I'll protect you for ever."

Close by, a champagne cork popped, coupes were filled and the happy couple toasted. Lucy took a photograph of them, then slipped up to her room to phone the news through to the *Chronicle* before changing for dinner. Her editor had been forbearing about the lack of information on the guest who had fallen from a balcony, but a film star's engagement was another matter entirely. As she'd said to Gina, if the paper wasn't the first to know, Phoebe would be out on her ear.

That task out of the way, Lucy gave herself up to wondering what Gustav had chosen for Myrtle. Perhaps she would find out tomorrow.

CHAPTER FIFTEEN

"Is it me," said Charles, looking around the grand reception hall where elegantly dressed guests were being served pre-dinner cocktails, "or are there even more waiters than usual tonight?"

The Bay Sands Hotel was certainly buzzing. Jack exchanged nods across the room with his bridge-playing acquaintances, grateful that the noisy crush prevented him and Charles from joining them. "There are," he said. "Lucy tells me some of the men who used to work here have come back for the occasion to help out."

"Interesting," mused Charles. "They arrive at Immingham with a contract for employment here, move on after a few weeks to work that suits them better, but are sufficiently grateful to the hotel to return as soon as an all-hands-on-deck call goes out. It doesn't sound like exploitation, does it?"

"No, especially as a number of them are interested in settling in Kingsthorpe permanently in this new housing project of Mackenzie's."

"I hope they are going to give Pyotr the design of the roof pitches."

"They may give him the design of the whole estate. It would be cheaper than employing a British architect."

"And he could include lots of cosy Russian touches to make the émigrés feel at home."

Jack laughed as if they were bandying the usual social platitudes. "But what do the consortium get out of it? That's what I can't understand. A few houses sold outright and the building costs for the others dribbling back in rent at a few shillings a week? Philanthropy has never figured in Edward Carter's business dealings before."

"They do say there's a first time for everything."

Jack gave a disbelieving snort. "We may work it out eventually. Meanwhile, Uncle Bob has asked Lucy to take as many photos as she can of waiters she doesn't recognise to send down to the Yard. I don't think he's ready to give up on the idea they're setting up a gang to challenge the status quo in the capital."

Charles shook his head. "Criminal gangs wasn't the impression I got from my various bouts of eavesdropping."

"No, but you were listening to the ones who are staying on here. There has to be a reason why Carter is intent on making life agreeable for them. It's keeping me awake at nights."

"As one old friend to another, allow me to point out that sentiment might be more effective with someone who doesn't have to listen to you snoring."

The crowd thinned momentarily and shifted. Across the intervening space, Jack met Lucy's eyes and raised his glass to her. She blushed and lined up another shot. He noticed Mrs Lester glance sharply at her, then turn to look at him. He'd been right. Nothing much got past her.

"Lucy isn't going to keep her rendezvous in the pavilion, then?" asked Charles.

"She is not," he said, feeling himself bristle.

His friend chuckled. "Every time."

"I would have thought," said Jack, "that you had enough to do this evening without trying to get a rise out of me."

"But it is so amusing. I can do it while I watch the waiters for hidden messages."

"You are supposed to be watching Karlsson as well."

"I will, just as soon as he puts in an appearance."

Jack idly scrutinised the glittering crowd. "Has he not? That's odd. Forrest and the Mackenzies are here, playing the affable hosts. Most of the other top-floor residents are circulating too. I can't see my uncle and Maynard yet. Delaney offered them the hospitality of the hotel with as good a grace as he could manage. They thanked him and said they'd use Hilliard's room to change so it wouldn't be obvious to the guests that there were rozzers on the premises."

"And people say our police are unsympathetic. What ho, a space is being cleared at the bottom of the staircase. I deduce a fashion sensation is about to descend. And Phoebe Sugar moving into place to photograph her, right on cue. Now I understand why we have all been kept milling around out here."

Charles was right, realised Jack. Edward Carter came down the grand staircase first and stood waiting by the curved handrail for his daughter. He seemed, by sheer force of will, to have summoned Lord Elvedon to wait on the other side. With superb assurance, Veronique Carter descended, step by leisurely step, to join them.

It was a memorable entrance. Her strapless sheath was midnight blue, gloving her in expensive, deceptive simplicity. Her French-heeled sandals winked with sapphires. Everyone's eyes, however, were riveted to the column of her throat where, held in a filigree cobweb of fine gold chains, blazed an enormous sunburst of diamonds. At the centre of the setting was...

"My God," breathed Jack. "That's the Kadensca Star."

Charles's indrawn breath confirmed it.

A waiter, arriving next to them with a tray of

champagne, nodded. "Da. Is a great stone. There would be much honour in the cutting of that one."

And like the tolling of a great bell, understanding reverberated in Jack's head. Oh, the sweet relief. "You are a lapidary?" he asked casually.

The man returned his gaze, limpid-eyed. "Me? I am waiter. More champagne?"

Jack replaced his empty glass with a full one from the tray. "But you were a lapidary once, yes?"

"A thousand years ago, perhaps. In a different life."

They have a top craftsman to run it.
Jabbering away in some foreign lingo.
An old, old stone in a new setting.

"And will be again, I think," said Jack.

The man shrugged. "Today I am waiter." He turned to Charles. "More champagne, sir?"

"Charles," said Jack as the waiter moved out of earshot. "How long has the Kadensca Star been lost?"

"Since the Russian revolution, along with countless other aristocratic jewellery collections."

"Do we at last think we know what is going on?"

"I believe we do."

"Thank the lord for that. Mostly gems - witness Mrs Mackenzie's bracelet and Gina's ring - but now and again a complete piece. And that is why the staff here are not Bolshevik gang members. That is why they are happy to work in Edward Carter's hotel and restore his run-down boarding houses while they wait for Mackenzie to build them homes of their own. They are ordinary Russian citizens in search of the life they used to live. The price for the crossing is to be a courier, nothing more nor less."

Charles exhaled with quiet satisfaction. "I agree. My lords and masters will be most relieved. They may want to drop a hint in the right ears that a certain amount of duty on the complete pieces would be appreciated, but I don't fancy their chances of getting it. All that will happen is that the consortium sets up business elsewhere." He met Jack's eyes. "I imagine that would not be in anyone's interests."

"Definitely not. Easier by far to keep an eye on an operation when you know where it is."

"I shall convey as much to headquarters. Not much of a story in it for you, is there?"

"Gem smuggling? Not as such, no, just another sideline to add to Carter's money-making empire. However, I can speculate on an aspect that might be a story."

"I'm all ears."

They were already speaking in low voices. Now Jack dropped to a murmur. "Picture Xavier Hilliard, driven by curiosity, low cunning and sheer native instinct to find out why Delaney's debt was suddenly repaid in full and why Delaney himself is about to move his family to the edge of nowhere. It does not take long to uncover Mr Carter's involvement in both circumstances. Hilliard senses a big, juicy, blackmail-worthy story. He sets his plans in motion and waits for an opportune moment. Now picture him eavesdropping on the consortium's business meeting and making the same discovery that we have just made."

"I'm with you so far," said Charles.

"He would have wanted a cut. No question. But for that he would need actual physical evidence, such as he might reasonably expect to find in Carter's suite."

Over by the stairs, Veronique led the way into dinner on Lord Elvedon's arm.

"Or perhaps," continued Jack, watching the satisfaction on Veronique's father's face, "Hilliard asked a different price for his silence. One that someone was not prepared to pay."

Lucy was passing over the latest rolls of film to Mr Curtis when Jack entered the small sitting room that the police had taken over. "I snapped as many waiters as I could," she said, "but they are in amongst my normal shots so I'll want them back. I need to send the society prints to the *Chronicle*."

"Fenn can make a duplicate set."

"Russian jewels," said Jack.

"Well, if you're offering..." said Lucy brightly.

"Would that I could afford them," he replied. "Charles has gone into dinner to keep an eye on our main players, but we have had a revelation."

Curtis looked up sharply, his expression suddenly very like his nephew's. "Expound," he invited.

"Both of us were struck all of a heap when Veronique Carter made her grand entrance, which is not a sentence I ever thought I'd hear myself saying."

"Jack, get on with it," urged Lucy.

"Russian jewellery is the reason for the Bay Sands Hotel's existence. There are fortunes in gems that have been concealed on country estates and the like since the revolution. The great houses were fabulously wealthy and the aristocratic émigrés didn't all get their riches out of the country in the scramble to save their own necks. My contention is that ordinary Russians are escaping in small groups to England, carrying some of those cached jewels with them as their escape price."

Lucy stared. "It's been ten years since the Russian revolution."

"There are still jewels hidden away. Once out of the country, they can release funds for their original owners. Those owners can't get them out themselves, but they can pass the location of their cache to a trusted fixer. There are always people desperate to leave. Sewing a handful of sapphires or a few loose diamonds into the hems of their coats as they cross Russia, Finland and Sweden to get to Britain is a small price to pay for freedom. They are provided with good quality passports and travel papers, a modest suitcase and a train fare. Everything is done very quietly. Once the courier gets here, their contract is fulfilled. My bet is that a percentage of each gem sale over here is put into a bank account in the fixer's name ready for the day when the motherland gets too hot for him and he smuggles himself out. The consortium, of course, also gets a percentage to parcel out between themselves. Meanwhile, the Bay Sands Hotel gets a ready supply of staff and the émigrés get work, papers, references and legal standing. The original owner will count themselves lucky to get half what the gems fetch."

"And all legal," said Curtis bitterly.

"Not quite. The reason Charles and I were rendered speechless at the sight of Veronique Carter is that the Kadensca Star - which has been lost for a decade - is currently adorning her neck in all its original glory."

"Is it now?"

"There would have been a tidy duty to pay on that if it had come through customs."

Lucy had a thought. "I wonder if that was what she was talking about yesterday? Irene and I assumed it was a dress she wanted to wear to her cocktail party that her father was vetoing, but it could have been the necklace. Mr Carter was saying it would have more of an effect at the ball."

"He was right about that," said Jack with a chuckle.

Curtis tapped his notes. "You are postulating that the gardeners and waiters and what-have-you were all couriers? It isn't illegal to import gems. Would they talk to us about it?"

Jack gave a derisory snort. "What do you think? Importing gems may be legal here, but I'm damn sure exporting them is illegal in Mother Russia. The Bolsheviks want all the pretty baubles for themselves to sell for arms. Nobody will say a thing. Don't forget most of Delaney's workforce will still have family over there."

"Pity," said Curtis. "I'd love to get something on Carter."

Jack's expression turned remote. "As would Xavier Hilliard. He was as suspicious of the set up here as you were, but his sights were set on profit. That's why he came to Kingsthorpe, why he was at such pains to get access to Lucy's room with its handy drainpipe to the top floor. If he had found out about the jewellery racket, it would have given the whole boiling lot of them a motive for his murder. Preferably before he got his hands on solid evidence."

"There were a lot of the Russians about indoors that day," said Lucy thoughtfully. "Waiters, maintenance men, busy in the corridors, popping in and out of the stairwell. I'm sure that ought to mean something."

Curtis looked sceptical. "It should, except the hand print on the wall outside your room and the partial fingerprints on the talcum powder tin and the jar of cream are unknown. Draper has taken prints from everybody in this hotel, and they don't match."

Jack stretched. "Back to the drawing board, then. May I take you into dinner, Miss Sugar?"

"That would be lovely. Is it wise?"

"I am beyond the point at which I care."

"All right, then. Are you eating as well, Mr Curtis?"

"I'm told a table will be provided. Maynard and the team will be back shortly. I'll wait for them. If you'd like to pop in here later you can collect your photographs."

Lucy preceded Jack into the reception hall. It would be nice to actually sit with him, to talk to him, even if it was as Phoebe. She turned to say as much and saw Gustav Karlsson shepherding a pretty young woman through from the Palm Court lounge. Lucy just had time to be outraged that it wasn't Myrtle on Karlsson's arm when she realised it *was* Myrtle. It was Myrtle transformed.

"Oh help," she said, and slid quickly into one of the deep chairs so her friend wouldn't recognise her.

Jack instantly sat on the arm of the chair, screening her. "Is the lady with the devoted expression who I assume she is?" he murmured.

Lucy shrank back further and bent her head as if searching the contents of her handbag. "Yes. That's Myrtle. She mustn't see me."

"I shouldn't worry. Someone else has just seen her and he doesn't look pleased."

Up until this point, Fauntleroy Delaney had been having an exceedingly good evening. His hotel was full to bursting point with the highest class of clientele. The bar was doing a brisk trade. The casino was busy. The kitchen - not that he went in there too often for fear of upsetting the chefs - was wreathed in the smells of succulent roasts and rich wine sauces. In the dining room, Mr Carter was beaming expansively, as well he might. His daughter was the sensation of the hour and surely the Earl of Elvedon must be on the point of proposing. Everyone was in good spirits, there was no Xavier Hilliard to make trouble and Grigory had even contrived a small table near the service door for the police, where they could be served with despatch and not listen in on any of the more important guests.

It was, therefore, a considerable shock, while perambulating contentedly through the reception hall, to come face to face with Karlsson and his partner. Only to realise that his partner was Myrtle!

"Myrtle," he said in outrage.

"Hello, Uncle Faun. It's a lovely party, isn't it?"

"What are you doing here?"

"Myrtle is my partner," said Gustav Karlsson, pleasantly but firmly. "In the future, I hope she will accompany me on many such occasions. She has done me the very great honour of agreeing to become my wife."

There was a roaring in Delaney's ears obliterating the sophisticated rise and fall of the guests' voices.

"Show your uncle your ring, my love," said Karlsson.

Myrtle blushed and held out her left hand for him to see. A cluster of sapphires sparkled on her finger. "Isn't it beautiful?"

Delaney's mouth dropped open in horror. The only reason he didn't howl his pain to the four winds was that he was surrounded by affluent clients. "I have been nurturing a snake in my bosom," he said in a trembling, wounded voice. "All the money and time I spent feeding and housing and training you and this is how you repay me."

Gustav repossessed himself of Myrtle's hand. "Then you should have paid her more and valued her more," he said calmly.

Delaney put a hand to his brow. "Who would have thought I'd been wary about the wrong man? *You* are the wolf, not Xavier. You have infiltrated my hotel and stolen the lamb from under my nose."

"Don't say that, Uncle Faun," said Myrtle, tears welling up in her eyes. "I wouldn't do anything to..."

"Hush, my love," said Karlsson tenderly. And to Delaney, "Be easy. You have had a shock and are upset because you cannot run the hotel at the present moment without Myrtle. I agree with you. She is a treasure beyond price. Reflect that you would also find it difficult to run it without me and my delivery service and my good will. I am not going to marry her out of hand, my friend.

There are many things to organise. There will be time enough to train up an assistant. Meanwhile, my Myrtle is most distressed that you are not after all fond enough of her to put her happiness above your own comfort and convenience."

His voice held an implacable note. Delaney looked from him to his niece and realised that the point at which he could have influenced her was gone. He forced a smile on to his face. "I am so sorry, Myrtle. I did not mean to upset you. As Gustav says, it was simply the surprise. Of course I wish you happy. All the happiness in the world." He fetched up a sentimental sigh. "You look so pretty tonight. Just like your mother when she was your age." This was an outright lie, but Myrtle beamed through her tears. "I will miss you very much," he added, which at least had the advantage of being the absolute truth.

Lucy, disregarded in the deep chair, widened her eyes. Jack laid a finger over his lips until all three of them had gone into the dining room.

"Mr Delaney called Hilliard the wolf," she whispered.

"He did indeed," replied Jack.

"The extra waiters, could the mystery hand print have been one of them?"

"The police will be checking. I don't see how, though. Unless Edward Carter got everybody he cared about out of the hotel, then left instructions for Hilliard to be followed all day with any opportunity to dispose of him to be seized if it arose."

"On my balcony?"

"That's the rub. I don't see how they'd know. Which is a pity because the whole operation does have his feel to it."

"It would never work. If Hilliard was as clever and dangerous as all that, he would realise he was being kept under observation. But I do agree everyone was got out of the way deliberately. Mr Carter even said, out loud at the reception counter when Hilliard was there, that the suite would be empty for the afternoon. An obvious lure to get Hilliard up there to search for evidence of the jewellery operation."

"We need to think some more. Shall we dine?"

In the doorway, they paused to let Thalia Portman and Mrs Lester politely vie for position.

"I hope you are quite well now," said Thalia Portman graciously.

Mrs Lester raised her eyebrows. "I am in perfect health, thank you."

Mrs Portman gave a knowing smile. "I assumed when I saw you in town the other week that you had been visiting your doctor. I have been trying out a new man. For my nerves, you know. He has the most advanced notions of treatment. Expensive, of course, as they all are, but well worth it." Her gaze wandered disparagingly over the compact, rotund form of Mr Lester. "Do let me know if you ever need his name. You won't regret it." And having rendered Mrs Lester speechless, she sailed victoriously into the dining room ahead of her.

Mrs Lester pursed her lips and took her husband's arm in order to find a table well away from the widow.

"What a giggle," said Amanda. "Mummy is never ill and when she is, she uses our family doctor at home. Mrs Portman just wanted to get to the table near the waiter's station. Honestly, she is dreadful."

"Theo," announced Julie, "if I ever get like her, I want you to promise to shoot me."

"Couldn't," said Theo simply.

"Oh, that's so sweet."

"Couldn't, because if you were like her, you'd be a widow and I'd be dead."

Behind them, Jack chuckled. "Never change, Theo."

But Lucy, putting the snatch of conversation together with her talk to Mrs Lester earlier in the week, was visited by a very odd notion. "I wonder," she said, "where Mrs Portman's doctor has his practice."

CHAPTER SIXTEEN

It became obvious as dinner progressed that Veronique Carter was no longer in the sunniest of humours. This was the grand opening celebration for her father's hotel, the triumphant culmination of a successful vision. Having expected to bask in his reflected glory all evening, she was darting increasingly venomous glances at the stream of people crossing to the Lester table to congratulate Gina Bianca on her engagement. Even in her own party, Myrtle and Gustav Karlsson were being toasted. It was perfectly plain to Lucy, looking across the intervening tables, that the thought of being eclipsed by the drab young woman from the office on this, *her* special night, had already brought the tobacco heiress to simmering point.

"Trouble there," murmured Jack to Charles, with a sideways tip of his head.

"Not for us," replied Charles. "But I'd say Rupert's days as a bachelor are numbered."

"Tonight, you think?"

"Definitely."

Lucy grimaced. That was a nuisance. Phoebe would have to be on hand to take a photo and phone the news through to the paper. She had been planning on sneaking back to the staff block before the grounds became too busy.

They were moving from the dining room to the Palm Court lounge when she felt a touch on her arm. Sergeant Fenn stood there.

"I beg your pardon, miss. The inspector would like a word."

Lucy groaned for the benefit of those nearby. "It'll be about my room again, no doubt."

As the door to the small sitting room closed behind her, she saw the photographic prints on the table.

"Oh, you've done all of them," she said. "How very kind of you, Sergeant Fenn."

"It was a pleasure. I didn't know which ones were ours, so to speak. Mr Curtis wants them as soon as possible. You take a nice composition. Good to see someone who doesn't waste film."

"Can't afford to," rejoined Lucy. They grinned at each other.

"There's only one where you seemed in more of a hurry than usual." Fenn slid out the photo of Ronnie Oaks. "Bit rushed, was it?"

"Yes. That is Mr Oaks. He was a visitor, not a guest. He told me on the first day here that he didn't like having his photograph taken. Jack thought Mr Curtis might be interested in finding out why."

Sergeant Fenn studied the face. "I don't recognise him, but we can send it down to the records office along with the others. That'll be a nice job for someone."

"There will be more by the end of this evening."

"If I'm still here when you've finished, I'll get them done for the morning."

"Thank you. I'm hoping I won't be late." Lucy went through the pile, separating her own photos from the ones for the police. She paused at the one of Gina and Charles dancing. Gina would be pleased with that, she thought. She'd been wearing a sleeveless silk sheath which showed up the admirable line of her body. Lucy noted absently that it had been before she hurt her arm. She riffled through to the photos she had taken on the jetty. Yes, Gina had cap sleeves on her dress here, and had deliberately eased them over her shoulders to hide the bruise. She looked happier in these, turning to laugh at Mr Ward, though he himself was out of shot. Lucy was obscurely relieved that she really did seem to love him. She'd come to like the troubled actress, it was nice to know Gina wasn't pretending just to get out of an abusive relationship.

Jack slipped into the room. "Have you got your camera?" he asked. "Rupert has just been jockeyed to the point of no return. Come on."

They returned to the Palm Court lounge where champagne corks were being drawn in a series of triumphant explosions and ranks of fresh glasses had made an appearance. Veronique Carter looked exultant. Edward Carter, receiving the congratulations of his business associates, looked sleek. The Earl of Elvedon looked as improbably handsome as ever and was admiring the image of himself and his bride-to-be in the glass on the wall. The aunts, Lucy noticed, merely looked thankful.

"Congratulations, Miss Carter," murmured Lucy, moving forward with her camera. "Congratulations, Lord Elvedon. May I take a photo for the *Chronicle*?"

"Of course," said Veronique graciously, and linked arms with her fiancé.

As well she might, thought Lucy. The sooner the news was splashed all over the papers, the more difficult Rupert would find it to wriggle out of the engagement.

She managed to get a few words from them expressing their happiness (chosen in advance in Miss Carter's case, she suspected) and slipped up to her room to phone the news through.

She'd intended going back to the staff block, but when

she came down without her camera, thinking she ought to let Jack know she was off, the orchestra had struck up a waltz for the happy couple. They were followed on to the floor by Gustav and Myrtle, then Gina Bianca and Jimmy Ward, who proved able to dance as efficiently as he played tennis.

"Shall we?" murmured Jack in her ear.

"Yes, please," said Lucy, and slipped sideways into her own small piece of heaven.

After the dance, Lucy found herself next to Gina. The actress regarded Veronique and Rupert critically. "Good luck to them. I think mine is the better deal though. She's got class, I'll give her that, but neither of them look as if they are adored, do they?"

"Oh, I don't know," said Lucy. "I'm pretty sure they each adore themselves."

"Xavier would have been wild," said Gina. "He wanted Miss Carter. She was going to be his passport to the upper classes."

That's what Jack had thought. "Mr Carter is a industrialist, not landed gentry," she pointed out. "That's why Miss Carter has been after the Earl of Elvedon. Mr Sinclair says marrying into the aristocracy has always been her goal."

Gina shrugged. "Money is what talked with Xavier. Enough of it and he could buy his own title."

"That's one way of looking at it. Did he say so? That he wanted Miss Carter?" Lucy tried to sound as if she was simply making conversation.

"He said there were ways and ways. Find the right lever and everything else gave way. I didn't care as long as the lever wasn't me. I reckon that was why he was so cross on Monday night. I reckon she'd snubbed him after that dance they had. He'd have hated that. He wasn't used to being turned down."

"Monday night?"

Gina looked shamefaced and lowered her voice. "I told you I never could resist him. I stayed in his room that night. He was fuming and wanted to feel better."

So that was why his bed had been in such disarray on Tuesday morning. "My lips are sealed," Lucy assured her.

"Thanks. It didn't mean anything, I was just handy. It didn't make him fall in love with me or anything. When I went back to my own room, he still followed me as far as the stairs to remind me to do what he'd said. You know, messing up your room so you'd want to swap."

The conversation in the stairwell. That's what it had been about. "Charming."

"That was Xavier. I can't believe I don't have to worry about him any more. It's like a dream come true."

"I ought to go," said Lucy to Jack after they'd had a further dance.

"I'll walk you across."

"I need to change first. You probably shouldn't walk me when I'm dressed as me."

"Can a man not saunter alone under the stars after a convivial evening?"

Luck chuckled, collected her photographs from the police, left tonight's films with Sergeant Fenn and went upstairs.

"I was thinking Phoebe should go back to London," she said as they exited via the side stairs. "There's nothing for her to stay for now."

"That's a shame."

"I'll still be here as me."

"I'd rather we were both here as ourselves," he grumbled, pulling her to him in the shadows.

"Jack, what if anyone sees us?"

"Who is going to... oh cripes."

Freed from his embrace, Lucy blinked. Under the influence of free-flowing champagne, the ball had spilled out from inside to take over the gardens. So much for slipping back unobserved. "Down this path," she said. "Keep to the wall. I can get into the staff wing once I'm past the pavilion."

"That's what you think. There appears to be a couple sitting on the bench, and not so engrossed in each other that they won't spot you."

"No guest is going to be interested in an off-duty chambermaid."

"I suppose not," said Jack with some reluctance. "Goodnight then."

The couple on the bench turned to each other and Lucy saw the woman's profile quite clearly in the moonlight. She whisked herself back into Jack's arms and pulled his head down to hers.

He made a gratified noise. "You could always stay with me again if you can't bear to let me go," he murmured.

"I'm going to have to. The woman on the bench is Irene, and I think the chap with her is Constable Williams."

"Morning," said Irene, stifling a yawn. "How was your half-day?"

Lucy was distinctly bleary-eyed. It was a good thing Phoebe was checking out today. She needed to catch up on her sleep. "I always enjoy time off. I looked at all the new shops, treated myself to a nice tea and watched a film." She made a face. "I also rang my mother. She wants me to go home. Never mind me, how was the ball? What did the ladies wear?"

She poured herself a cup of strong tea as she listened to Irene's description of the clothes and the jewels.

"It sounds wonderful. I did knock when I got back, but you didn't answer. Were you worn out doing up all their invisible fastenings?"

Irene flushed a dull red. "Not exactly. I came back here after the guests had gone down for dinner and saw Billy in the grounds. I chaffed him a bit and he told me he was keeping observation on the pavilion to see who went in so I ought to leave him to his job."

The pavilion. Lucy remembered guiltily that Phoebe had been supposed to meet someone there.

Irene was still talking. "I said anyone would see him a mile away and sheer off, and wouldn't it be better if he took off his helmet and sat on the bench with me like we were a regular couple. So we did and he told me how he likes being a copper and it's a good career with a pension, but he'd like to get on in the force. That might mean applying for a transfer and he was worried about not fitting in and being lonely if he was sent some place where he didn't know anyone. I said he'd make friends in no time if he worked to overcome his shyness, and besides, he must be lonely keeping watch out here, so where was the difference?"

Lucy grinned, thinking her friend would probably be very good for the young constable. "What did he say to that?"

"That he thought he was being kept out of the way for some reason."

Oh dear, that would be so he didn't see her as Phoebe inside the hotel. "Surely not. If he'd been entrusted with important observation, they must think well of him."

"That's what I said," replied Irene. "Anyway, he told me this case had put him right off applying to move into the plain clothes branch. He'd thought it might be interesting but after being roped in to help the Scotland Yard sergeants go over every inch of the side stairs, he says it's the most boring job in the world. The wall and the banister are covered in hand prints, apparently, and when it came to the Yard men getting excited about a few tiny holes in the skirting board, well, that did it. Billy said he's going to stick to the uniformed branch. There's more going on, even in Kingsthorpe."

"You seem to have had a nice chat, anyway. Did he see whoever he was supposed to be watching for?"

"No. We ended up sitting there all evening and we did keep watch, but no one came near. Mind you, the guests were all over the gardens, so maybe that's what put them off."

"It was certainly noisy outside," agreed Lucy. She grinned sideways at her friend. "When are you seeing him again, then?"

Irene met her overly innocent gaze with a wry grin. "Monday, my half day. He's going to borrow a car from a pal and take me and May to Skegness."

"Good morning, gentlemen. Your early tea."

"I'm going off your lady," said Charles without opening his eyes.

"She means well," said Jack. He was wearing a dressing gown and was seated at his table writing up notes. He snatched a quick kiss as she put the tray down. "What's the gossip from the servants' hall this morning?"

"The Russians are all highly delighted about Myrtle and Mr Karlsson. They like him and they approve of her and they seem to think he'll be blessed with a nursery full of little blond moppets in no time."

"They are probably right." Jack shuffled his pages together. "That's as much of last night's conversations as I can remember for Uncle Bob. I wish I had something to keep them together."

"I'll fetch you one of Phoebe's big envelopes. You couldn't go into town after breakfast and post her photos to the *Chronicle*, could you? The sooner they get there the better."

"Can't you give them to the chap on the desk to mail?"

She raised her eyebrows at him. "What, as Lucy?"

"Oh, I was forgetting."

"I'll do it," said Charles. "I'm off to Immingham again this morning. Orders from above. I knew it was a mistake phoning them yesterday."

"I'll get out of your way." She rummaged in her pocket. "Here, use this bit of fishing line for now, Jack. Guests are so careless. I found it on..." Her voice tailed off.

"Found it where?"

Even Charles opened one eye.

Lucy sat on the end of the bed with a thump. "I found it on the side stairs on Wednesday. Jack, Constable Williams told Irene that Fenn and Draper found holes in the skirting board on the stairs." *And the waiter stopped me running down them and more of them were in evidence the whole time I was up on the top floor.*

"And the Russians were swarming all over them," said Jack, echoing her thoughts. "It's the last piece of the puzzle. Carter was threatened - *'Let me marry your daughter or I blow the gaff'* - and decided to take Hilliard out. He probably fobbed him off, thus guaranteeing him looking for concrete proof in Carter's suite. He then ensured the top floor was vacant, had waiters standing by with near-invisible tripwires in case Hilliard used the side stairs, and protected himself and the staff by making sure no innocent person was hurt."

"But Hilliard *didn't* use the stairs. How would Mr Carter have known about the drainpipe and his athletic skills? He wouldn't have had time to dig into his past."

Jack rubbed his nose. "He has money. Other people do the digging for him."

"You'll never prove it."

"Oh ye of little faith. I can dig too. I'll tell Uncle Bob about this as soon as he gets here. Leave me the fishing line. Off you go and be a chambermaid."

Lucy spent most of the next hour working out how soon she could check Phoebe out of the hotel and then tender her own resignation.

"I thought you'd be spending your break downstairs congratulating Myrtle," said Irene, coming into the cubby and flopping into a chair.

Lucy leapt up. "Oh, how awful. I completely forgot."

"That's not like you."

Because I already knew. And I forgot I wasn't supposed to know. Lucy cast about for an excuse and found one that fitted perfectly. "I'm not thinking straight. I'm worried about my mother. She doesn't usually ask me to go home just like that. It's mostly heavy hints. I'd better write this afternoon. Oh dear, Myrtle will be terribly hurt if I don't pop in. I'll dash down now."

She ran down the stairs, reflecting that there weren't any Russians to tell her to slow down today. Why hadn't she realised at the time how odd that had been?

"Oh, thank you," said Myrtle when she slid past Quentin on the counter and into her friend's office. She held out her hand. "Look, isn't it beautiful?"

"It's a gorgeous ring. You are so lucky. And you really attended the ball?"

"I really did. I'm dying to tell you about it. Can you come out for lunch? Gustav has gone to Immingham to let his crew know their passage back will be delayed. Only until Monday, but it gives us a couple of days to start organising things."

Lucy hesitated, but Myrtle was evidently desperate

to sing her fiancé's praises so she agreed. At least she wouldn't feel so bad about abandoning her friend to continued servitude when she went back to London. Gustav Karlsson would see she wasn't exploited any more.

"Thanks," beamed Myrtle. "Uncle Faun is being really nice about it. It's lovely when everyone's happy, isn't it?"

"Lovely," said Lucy weakly.

Jack called in on his uncle soon after breakfast to give him the length of fishing line Lucy had found on the stairs and to tell him the conclusions they had drawn.

Curtis grunted. "You call them conclusions. I call them conjecture. I'm not saying you're wrong, but I'll have to see all these people again and I know exactly what will happen. I will ask each of the staff if they had anything to do with attaching tripwires to drawing pins and they will all look at me as if I'm an escaped mental patient and say no. Still less will they implicate anyone else."

Maynard grinned. "It fits though. You can't say it doesn't fit. I'll get along to the Kingsthorpe police station and ring the Yard for the latest reports. They might have matched some fingerprints, you never know. I'll be back by the time you want to interview Carter and his consortium."

Curtis shook his head. "They'll never talk. It's not worth rattling them at this stage. One of the Russians might crack."

Which left Jack kicking his heels and giving serious thought to his next move. Having settled to his own satisfaction why Carter and his associates were investing in the Bay Sands Hotel, there didn't seem much more reason for him to be here. It wasn't a story he could use, and pretending to be one of the idle rich instead of working to make the world better was driving him to breaking point. In this unsettled state of mind, he decided to go for a bracing swim in the bay. He was treated to a very hard stare from the chambermaids' cubby on his return to his room.

"Well done," said Lucy, coming in some fifteen minutes later with her cleaning basket. "I've just had a lovely disgruntled mutter with Irene about thoughtless young men who go sea-bathing early and then mess up their bathrooms washing the brine off themselves so I have to clean again before the housekeeper comes around."

"I only did it so I can talk to you. I'm going to tell Uncle Bob I'm going back to London. As far as I can see, we've found out what we came here to do. The hotel is here because it is handy for Karlsson and because Edward Carter wants a seaside town to call his own. He wants his own craftsmen to rival anything found in London and he wants to build them nice houses to keep them here. Apart from being funded by smuggled jewels, the Kingsthorpe project seems to be on the level. End of story."

"And Xavier Hilliard?"

"That's where the Yard and I differ. They want proof, whereas I am quite happy with gut instinct. I can see why you don't write clever policemen into your books. There would be nothing for your amateur sleuths to do."

"The police are jolly useful for checking records and doing the routine questioning," said Lucy, wiping around the bath and expertly rinsing it clean. "There, that's done. One thing about this job, cleaning the flat is going to take no time at all once I'm home again." She gave him a rapid kiss. "Which can't come too soon for me. I'm lunching with Myrtle, by the way. She wants to tell me all about her engagement. See you later."

CHAPTER SEVENTEEN

Cheered by this episode, Jack settled down to work on the riddle of Xavier Hilliard's death for an hour to see where he might look for the proof his uncle craved. He studied the timetable, searching for a gap, a square not filled in. His finger stopped next to Mrs Lester. He didn't see how it would help, but it was a puzzle yet to be unravelled. She had deliberately kept Lucy away from her room on Tuesday afternoon whilst Xavier had been climbing the drainpipe. Just what had her connection with Hilliard been?

He sauntered downstairs. Mrs Lester was writing a letter in the lounge, surrounded by other ladies doing similar. He couldn't intrude, and even if he did, she would be unlikely to give anything away. Jack had a very high opinion of her intelligence.

His gaze fell on Thalia Portman, sitting by the door drumming her fingers on the small table next to her. Jack steeled himself.

"Are you going out for a drive?" he asked, indicating her furs and exquisite outdoor shoes. "May I join you while we both wait? My friend appears to have forgotten the time."

She swivelled to direct an assessing look at him. "Certainly. Mr Sinclair, isn't it? I do not know what has become of my driver."

Probably still at the garage, desperately drawing lots with all the other drivers for the honour of not taking her out. "It's as well there is always something to do here. Do you care for a hand of cards? Piquet, perhaps? Or écarté?"

Now he had her full attention. "You play écarté?"

"Learnt it in the cradle," said Jack, fetching a pack of cards from the shelf and deftly slipping out all cards below the seven while he was talking. "We had a French nursery maid. Made a fortune from the other servants and now runs her own casino."

She gave a slight smile. "Very well."

Thalia Portman - as Jack already knew - played a shrewd game. As soon as he proved her was her equal, he was able to introduce a few pertinent questions into the conversation.

"I once played whist against that fellow who died," he said. "He wasn't as good as he thought. Did you know him?"

"Briefly," said Thalia, exchanging four of her cards. "He was interested in looking around my suite, or so he said."

"It's one excuse," murmured Jack, with a glance of admiration.

Her smirk told him she'd understood his comment. "We toyed with the idea of the roof garden, but people are such prudes, even these days. My first husband and I used to play écarté for items of clothing on the terrace of his chateau and no one turned a hair."

"I can see that would add spice to the game, but I imagine the manager would prefer it if we stick to shilling points down here in the reception hall." He exchanged one of his own cards and waited for her to lead or exchange again. "You were lucky in your choice of spouse. I can't see Mrs Lester, for example, doing the same at their country house."

"King of trumps," declared Thalia. "That woman, such a hypocrite." She laid down a card.

Jack added one to her score. "Really? In what way?"

"Pretending she didn't know what I was talking about when I passed her going into my own doctor's building."

Jack adroitly lost the trick. "Oh, is that the doctor with the unconventional therapy method you mentioned? It sounded fascinating."

"Exactly. If anyone needs loosening up it's Mrs Lester."

Jack won the next trick, then led a card which - if he'd judged right - should give her the rest of the hand. "The reason I was interested is that my cousin was telling me his good lady isn't as forthcoming as he would like her to be. I wonder if it's any use her going to this doctor of yours?"

"Certainly. Dr Polyaki, Harley Street. Can't fail." She took the next three tricks in quick succession.

"Thank you. I'll pass that on to him. This looks like your driver." He paid her the winnings with a good grace and made his escape.

At one o'clock, Lucy was once more dressed in her boxy jumper and skirt and her blue beret, waiting in the switchboard alcove for Myrtle to finish work.

Rupert's aunts were checking out with the satisfaction of a job well done, Mr Carter, Veronique and Lord Elvedon had just gone through to the dining room, Gina Bianca and Jimmy Ward were sitting with their heads together in the Palm Court lounge. Jack crossed the busy reception hall and managed his customary trick of sliding into the small sitting room without anyone but her noticing.

"I'm ready," said Myrtle, pulling on her gloves and tucking her arm into Lucy's as they went through the plate glass doors.

It was a nice day for a walk, crisp and fresh with the breeze blowing in from the sea. Lucy felt a twinge of foreboding as she saw Mr Oaks coming towards them. He was striding along fast, his head down and thrust forward as if he was charging an invisible barrier. She pulled Myrtle hastily out of the way, saying, "Oh dear, Mr Oaks has turned up. That's a pity. Miss Bianca has been looking so happy the last couple of days."

Fortunately, Myrtle didn't question how her friend knew the state of mind of a guest on a different floor. Instead she stopped. "He's here again? Well, he can't go in. Two of the guests have made a formal complaint about him. They were terribly upset by his behaviour. Uncle Faun has barred him from the hotel."

Before Lucy could prevent it, she had run back and pulled at Mr Oaks's jacket to get his attention. "I'm sorry, sir, but you can't go into the hotel."

He swung around in amazement. Lucy could understand that. She was pretty amazed herself. Being in love had certainly emboldened Myrtle.

"Who is going to stop me?" he said. "I've got business with Miss Bianca."

Lucy hurried up, taking care to keep her beret pulled low over her forehead. "You really can't, sir," she said in a scared voice, quite unlike her own. "The police are everywhere because of one of the guests falling off the balcony. We work there, so we know."

"Is that so?" There was an ugly rasp to his voice. "Then you can go and get Miss Bianca and we'll have our business talk out here. And just to make sure you do, your friend can keep me company until you get back." He gripped Myrtle's arm so hard she cried out in pain. He gave it a savage twist. "Watching? Just a sample of what I can do. No funny business. Go inside, give Miss Bianca the message and come straight out or it will be the worse for your pal."

His right fist closed menacingly. Lucy didn't need to

raise her eyes to see the fury pulsating out of him. He was six foot two to her friend's five foot nothing and at that moment, she could quite easily picture him dashing Myrtle to the ground like a china figurine and ploughing into the hotel, felling anyone who got in his way. He'd looked exactly the same way on Wednesday.

Lucy gasped as sharply as if she was the one having her arm twisted.

Wednesday.

Mr Oaks had been heading upstairs that day. She remembered his wet sleeve as he shoved past her, meaning he must have been standing within earshot of the reception counter. She remembered Mr Carter had just announced that his suite was going to be vacant all afternoon and that Xavier Hilliard was clearly visible behind him.

She also remembered that Gina had at one point had Hilliard's pass key. "I'll fetch her," she whispered nervously and scuttled inside.

Indoors, she rushed straight to the lounge. Thankfully, Gina was still there.

"Excuse me, Miss Bianca. Can I have a word, please?" she said.

Gina turned with a smile, ready to sign an autograph. Her eyes widened as she recognised Lucy. "Phoebe?" she said, confused.

Lucy drew her to one side. "Yes, I'm Phoebe, pretend you haven't noticed. This is really important, Gina. Whatever you do don't go outside. Mr Oaks is out there baying for your blood."

"Ronnie?" said Gina, her colour ebbing away.

"He's demanding to see you and threatening one of the staff. I'm about to tell the police. Listen, Gina, quick. When you explained to Mr Oaks about Mr Hilliard and the photographs, did you tell him what Hilliard used to do when you first knew him?"

Gina looked at her blankly. "Yes, of course. I gave him the whole story. He'd never have believed me otherwise. He'd have thought I was making it up so I could be on my own for a week. I had to show him how vile and manipulative Xavier could be."

Lucy nodded. It was all falling into place. "One more question. Did you give him the pass key?"

"He took it. He burst into my room on Wednesday, hit me on the arm, wrenched my handbag out of my hands and shook it upside down until the pass key fell out. Then he told me to get down to the courts and watch the tennis and keep my mouth shut. He said he was going to sort this out for good, and when he had, he'd be back for me and I was to think about what damage he could do to me if I annoyed him again. I was terrified."

"Thanks. Stay here. Don't say a word."

Oaks. It had been Oaks all along. He was the only person apart from Gina who knew for sure that Hilliard used to be an acrobat.

Lucy hurtled back into the reception hall and across to the small sitting room. She needed to find Jack. She needed to rescue Myrtle.

"Done all your questioning, then?" Jack asked his uncle, shutting the sitting room door quietly behind him.

"No. Go away."

"I was only going to enquire if a certain Dr Polyaki practised in the same building as Xavier Hilliard."

Curtis cocked an eye at him. "I can find out. Why?"

Jack told him. "If he does, it lends colour to our theory that Hilliard instructed Mrs Lester to keep Lucy busy on Tuesday afternoon when he climbed up the drainpipe to listen to Carter's meeting."

"Your point?"

"That Hilliard may have had a hold on Mrs Lester, one she wanted to dissolve. The Lesters' room is immediately above Lucy's. She might easily have seen him on one of his other forays. Even if she didn't, she's a very clever woman and may have guessed what he was doing."

"Her own balcony is free of Hilliard's prints. How would she gain access to Lucy's room?"

Jack shrugged. "You're the detective, not me. She could have borrowed a spare key off the board. I'm only trying to be helpful."

Maynard came in, putting his hat and gloves down on the table. "The letter to Miss Sugar was left at reception by Hilliard himself," he reported. "His prints are on the envelope and on one edge of the paper. Giving himself another time slot to get into Carter's suite, presumably, in case the afternoon was a washout. On a more positive note, our boys have found reams of useful paperwork in Hilliard's safe."

"Good. Now we need to match it up with guests at the hotel. You gave them the list of residents?"

"I did. They were delighted to have so much extra to do to brighten their working hours."

Curtis snorted with amusement. "So nice to be able to spread a little joy. What else is going on in London? Are they managing without us?"

"We're a man down on the Harley Street surveillance team. Our chap was on the early shift in the café over the road when one of the customers caused a bit of a fracas. He was reading the newspaper over his breakfast and suddenly leapt up yelling that he'd bloody kill him. So our chap walks across to calm him down - which he'll be getting some advice about as it's the first item in the distraction techniques manual - gets laid out cold with a left hook and chummy lights off."

"That'll teach him not to neglect his physical fitness."

Jack grinned and was about to slip back into the reception hall as quietly as he'd entered when the door suddenly flew open and Lucy erupted into room.

"Come quick," she said. "Quick! It's an emergency! Oaks is outside holding Myrtle hostage until I fetch Gina."

Jack's muscles tensed. "What?"

"Ronnie Oaks. He did it. Killed Hilliard. He must have done. He's mad with jealousy over Gina and he knew about Hilliard being an acrobat. He took the key Hilliard had given Gina and told her he was going to sort him out once and for all. I even saw him going up the stairs. He sabotaged the drainpipe and the ledge and headed down to London to look for the naked photographs of her that Hilliard had. It all fits. It must have been him."

Curtis was already on his feet. "Proof?" he asked.

"I've proof he took the key. Gina will tell you about the conversation. His fingerprints will do the rest."

Maynard moved to the door. "I'll ring the station and get reinforcements."

"There's no time," said Lucy urgently. "He's got Myrtle in some sort of arm lock outside. I can delay him for a few moments, no more."

"We can't rush him on a supposition."

"He's got hold of Myrtle. That isn't a supposition. He's threatening her!"

Curtis and Maynard exchanged glances. "The moment he sees us he'll be off. Has he got a weapon?"

"I don't know." Lucy swung to Jack imploringly. "Think of something, Jack. Hurry."

Jack had already been thinking. Lucy's appeal, directly to him, sent a kick of fire into his soul. Purpose flooded into him. "The Russians," he said, snapping his fingers. "Didn't you say they like Karlsson? They won't stand for Myrtle being threatened. We'll tell Grigory that the man who the police think may have set the trap for Hilliard has got Myrtle outside and to mobilise the staff. They can come around in a flanking movement and prevent him getting away."

"I can't say anything of the sort to them," objected Curtis. "It's all conjecture."

"You can't," said Jack grimly. "I can. Go out there and delay him, Lucy. I'll be as quick as I can. For God's sake, don't take any risks."

She gave him a tight smile. "I won't. Don't be too long."

Jack didn't wait for his uncle's or Maynard's consent. He made straight for the dining room and the waiters' station. "Grigory," he said. "Myrtle needs your help."

Ninety seconds later he strolled outside, the very picture of an aimless young man sampling the sea air before going indoors for a spot of lunch. In front of him Lucy was hobbling and holding a hand to her side as if she had a stitch.

Jack had excellent hearing. He saw Oaks stride towards Lucy towing Karlsson's partner from last night along with him. The young woman's face was streaked with tears. Jack felt his blood boil.

"Well?" growled Oaks.

"Please, sir," said Lucy. "Miss Bianca is coming. I'm sorry it took so long. I had to look for her all over the hotel. Can Myrtle and I go to lunch now?"

Behind them, taking the long route around from behind the hotel, came an assortment of waiters, gardeners and chefs, moving silently in a purposeful line. With any luck there were more out of sight near the sharp end of the building, ready to cut Oaks off from the Skegness road should he make a bolt for it.

Oaks laughed at Lucy in disbelief. "Let you go? With police in the hotel? Not until I have Miss Bianca standing here where your little friend is now."

"But that's not fair," said Lucy, her voice rising. "We don't get long for lunch and you're going to make us late. Myrtle might lose her job over it."

Oaks's face changed, his attention sharpening. "Here," he said suspiciously. "Wait half a minute. Don't I know you? What's your game, eh?"

And that, as Jack admitted later, was where a perfectly good, if hastily planned, operation went out of control. The staff were in a loose line, moving quietly, working their way closer. Lucy was keeping Oaks's attention on her and Myrtle so he wouldn't look behind him and realise what was happening. Jack himself, along with the Scotland Yard detectives, were ready to rush him from the front as soon as it became necessary.

And then Oaks made the mistake of letting go of Myrtle and grabbing Lucy with an ugly look on his face.

Lucy told Jack afterwards that she'd never in her life seen anyone move as fast as he did then. He didn't consciously remember any of it. All he knew was the sensation of his feet pounding down the drive and of his fist crashing into Oaks's jaw to knock him senseless.

The first thing he heard when the roaring in his ears subsided, was his uncle's voice as he and Maynard hauled Oaks upright and handcuffed him.

"Mr Ronald Oaks? I'm Chief Inspector Curtis of Scotland Yard. I wonder if you wouldn't mind accompanying Inspector Maynard and myself to the police station to answer a few questions. There is a car coming to collect us now. I should warn you that anything you say will be taken down and may be used in evidence..."

Lucy and Myrtle were borne tenderly away by the Russians to be fussed over and given lunch in the staff dining room. They were delayed by Delaney who patted his niece's shoulder and said she'd been very brave and enquired in an anxious undertone whether Miss Sugar had got hold of the story.

"She said this morning that she was planning to go shopping," replied Lucy, clearly enough for Jack to hear.

"Ah," said Delaney, pleased. "No doubt she is lunching in Kingsthorpe. Good. Some publicity we can do without."

Jack gave a sardonic smile and watched Lucy disappear into the inner corridors of the hotel. He had to stop himself following her. Instead he joined his fellow guests in the hotel's strangely depleted dining room, where waiters were now hurrying back into position.

Gina Bianca stood in a rush and came over to him. "Thank you so much, Mr Sinclair. Won't you sit with us?"

Theo Nicholson looked up from his plate of beef. "Nice punch, Jack. Did you know the blighter?"

Julie and Amanda made cooing noises. "Where's Phoebe? She missed your heroic rescue of that poor girl. A lovely chance to impress her, wasted."

"She went shopping, I understand," said Jack, taking care not to meet Gina's eyes. "The manager is most relieved."

"Theo says the police have arrested Ronnie," said Gina. "Will they charge him for threatening that poor girl? What will happen when they let him go?"

This time Jack couldn't help but look at her. Had she really not worked it out? What did she think Oaks had been doing with that pass key on Wednesday?

Jimmy Ward finished clearing his plate and entered the conversation. "That's a very good point, Gina," he said seriously. "I believe you and I should toddle off back to town and get married straight away. The afternoon train will get us there nicely in time for dinner."

"Oh," said Gina faintly. "All right."

"I thought the police said none of us were to leave," remarked Jack.

"If the police want to talk to Gina, they can do it in town," said Jimmy. "I'll tell Mr Lester we're going and then I'll settle your bill, Gina. I expect you'll need a little while to pack. My sisters always do."

CHAPTER EIGHTEEN

In the staff dining room, Lucy allowed everyone to make a fuss of her and Myrtle, but was careful to be quieter than usual.

Eventually, Irene noticed. "What's the matter? Has it shaken you up?"

Lucy nodded. "Reaction, I expect. And also, I keep thinking about my mother. What if something bad had happened and the last conversation I'd had with her was me not offering to go home when I *knew* it sounded as if there was something wrong?"

"Ring her up. Florence will put it through from the switchboard if you ask."

Lucy looked shocked. "I couldn't do that. I'll go along to the garage and use the phone box there."

"Want me to come with you?"

"No, I'll be all right. Besides, you're dying to go into town and tell your own mum about the excitement, aren't you?"

Irene grinned. "I am a bit."

"I'll see you later then."

She slipped away from the table, to reappear n the other side of the hotel in due course as Phoebe.

Jack was on his balcony waiting for her. "Hello, you.

Did you bring any sensible shoes for Phoebe? Do you want to come for a walk?"

"I didn't, but I do. If I get blisters, you can carry me back."

"Fair enough. Manly heroics seem to be all I'm good for."

Lucy studied him. Where had that come from? "I *was* going to pack and check out. It's time Phoebe went home. I'm finding it very difficult to carry on with this, Jack."

He nodded. "Me too. Never again do we accept a commission from Uncle Bob that means we have to work separately. Come out with me now and pack after your towel stint. You don't want to risk pretending to catch the same train as Jimmy Ward and Gina Bianca."

"Oh, are they leaving? Good. Gina recognised me as Phoebe. I wouldn't bet on her forgetting she's not supposed to know anything and letting it slip to a table full of chattering socialites."

He gave a reluctant grin. "Why did you go straight to her? Why didn't you tell Uncle Bob first?"

She looked at him in surprise. "Gina was in danger! She might have gone outside at any moment. Warning her was vital."

"At the expense of your cover?"

"Yes, of course."

He was silent for a moment. "Fetch your coat. Let's go for that walk."

By common consent, they strolled along the road towards Kingsthorpe. Lucy eyed Jack sideways. She'd got the impression that his playboy image had been fretting him this week. He hadn't been edgy and restless when they were crossing the Atlantic and he'd been acting a part then as well. Unless it was her, unless he was resenting having fallen in love with her? She re-examined the memory of him powering along the path to slam his fist into Mr Oaks's jaw. No, that hadn't been faked. It must be something else.

"What's the matter, Jack?"

"I don't know. I'm confused. It was horrible letting you go off for lunch without me earlier. I wanted to consign the rest of the world to outer darkness and sweep you back to your flat in London and lock us both in for a fortnight."

The agreeable image this presented sent heat flickering through her. She tucked her arm into his. "That would be nice," she said. "Can we do it anyway? I've been wondering whether part of the problem this week has been that we don't properly know each other yet."

"I know I love you. I know when I hit Oaks I felt more in command of myself than at any point since I arrived in Kingsthorpe."

She smiled. "You have no idea how it made *me* feel. I love you too. What I meant is we haven't had enough time together. We know about deep feelings, but not the everyday ones. Would you be happy to sit on the sand and talk about books until the sun went down, for example? Would you be content to work at one end of the balcony while I worked at the other and never say a word to each other all morning?"

He nodded. "Yes, and yes, but I do see what you mean. Well then, how soon can we start? Presumably Lucy-the-chambermaid is staying on, even if Phoebe checks out."

"Not for much longer. She's currently ringing home to discover that her mother is terribly ill. I thought she might leave some time over the weekend."

"Good. Charles and I won't be far behind you. With any luck, we can all go together. And once we are back in London, there will be no more deception."

"Apart from you still being undercover reporter Jonathan Curtis and me being secret detective novelist Leonora Benson."

"If people knew about me, I'd soon not have a job at all. For the rest though... Lucy, I want to take you out. I want us to be known as a couple. I want to get invitations addressed to Mr Jack Sinclair and Miss Lucy Brown."

"I'd like that. With the exception of the Lester twins' double wedding. Though I rather suspect Mrs Lester has already torn up the contract from the *Chronicle*."

"Because Xavier Hilliard is no longer around to make things awkward for her, you mean? It must have been him she was giving that dirty look to that first evening, not Gina at all. I'd love to know what he had on her."

"There's investigative journalism and there's nosiness, Jack."

He grinned. "One often leads to another in my experience. Is that a police station I see before us? Shall we call in and bring ourselves up to date?"

"Before we do... we're assuming the prints on the wall and on Phoebe's lavender cosmetics belong to Oaks. If not, there will be more investigation needed."

Jack shook his head. "Not by us. We've found out what we came for, and none of it can we use. I want to get on with some real work. There's a nightclub in Soho that is starting to be frequented by some unexpected people."

"And I've got a whole notebook of ideas for the next Leonora Benson *and* the next career-girl story. There's the bus. I'll catch it back to the hotel and pack. See you at towel time."

In the police station, Jack was shown into a tiny office where he found his uncle. "Lucy and I are going back to London," he said. "Even if it was Edward Carter who set it all up and not Oaks at all, there's nothing useful we can do now."

"It was Oaks who laid the trap all right. The prints on

the wall and the balcony and the talcum powder tin and the jar of cream all match his, and he's been muttering obscenities about Hilliard and Miss Bianca ever since he regained consciousness. He's under guard at the hospital, by the way. You broke his jaw. However, I do agree with you that Carter set up a tripwire scenario. In the event, it wasn't used."

Maynard squeezed into the room. "Report from Harley Street. That photo we sent down on the overnight train of Oaks - he's been identified as the chap who laid out our man, so that's another charge to add to the sheet."

"Good." Curtis glanced at Jack. "You asked about Mrs Lester earlier on. I queried the team looking through the paperwork. Hilliard didn't have anything on her, unless you count *him* paying *her* for society information as something?"

Jack whistled, impressed. "The devil he did. That woman is extraordinary. I suppose it does cost a bit to catch a couple of viscounts for both your daughters in the same year. No wonder she wasn't amused when he turned the tables and threatened to spill the beans unless she put in an appearance here."

"That's all by the by. More to the point is that Oaks was also seen in Harley Street on the day of Hilliard's fall. Witness has him exiting the building just as our chaps were entering it. You'll remember we said there had been a break in."

"He was searching for the compromising photos of Gina," said Jack. "He grabbed her key, shook the talcum powder on the drainpipe, cursed at the wind, slapped a dollop of cream on the ledge, caught the London train and got to Hilliard's office before the alarm was raised here. He took a risk."

Curtis shook his head. "Not that much of a risk. It was only you ringing me as soon as you found the body that alerted us. In the normal course of events, he'd have had several more hours."

"And if Hilliard spotted the booby trap, Oaks would still have time to find the photos and cancel his hold on Gina. Even so, he was lucky. Due to Edward Carter, that side of the hotel was virtually untenanted."

"Yes. It grieves me immeasurably that our tobacco tycoon is once again untouchable."

"That's life. See you later." Jack went back outside. Kingsthorpe lay in front of him. He felt restless and unsatisfied. Maybe Lucy was right and what was needed was some simple, normal, everyday time with her. Suddenly he couldn't face another aimless afternoon. A familiar figure on the other side of the road caught his eye. Jack smiled to himself and followed him.

The walk had done Jack good, decided Lucy. He and Charles were both sprawled on their beds looking thoroughly at ease before going down for dinner. She took off her mob cap and sat on one of the chairs by the window.

"So, there you have it," said Jack. "We believe Edward Carter did plan to take Hilliard out because he'd made an ultimatum about marrying Veronique or he'd grass on their little operation. However, Oaks saved everyone the trouble by doing the deed. Oaks knew how Hilliard intended reaching the roof. There was no other way of getting into Carter's suite and laying his hands on firm evidence."

"None of the Carter information is provable," murmured Charles.

"Then how do you know?" asked Lucy.

Charles smiled enigmatically. "Let's just say I didn't waste my time on the trip back from Immingham with Gustav Karlsson."

"Mr Karlsson has already been upstairs to find me to thank me for preserving Myrtle and to invite me to the wedding," said Lucy ruefully. "I had to tell him I was returning home almost at once to be a dutiful daughter." She glanced at Jack. "I've packed Phoebe's bag. I'm hoping to leave as myself tomorrow. I need to see Mrs Ryland as soon as I've finished here. Irene says she knows a girl who might take my place."

"What are you going to do with Phoebe's luggage?" asked Charles.

She turned her head and looked thoughtfully at his massive trunk. "It might fit in there?"

He sighed. "Go and get it."

She did so. Then said, "So the Russians are in the clear on all counts? Good. I'm glad. It was horrible of Mr Carter to try to use them."

Charles nodded. "Yes, they won't be bothered any more as long as they keep their heads down and themselves out of trouble, which they will because of the plans to turn Kingsthorpe into a pleasant enclave for them and their families."

"Little Russia, sponsored by Edward Carter," drawled Jack.

"I doubt anyone will look too closely at the stamp of entry on their passports. It's red, it looks official, they have their contract of employment. It may even *be* official as the chap who comes out to Karlsson's boat is a genuine immigration officer. If not, no one is going to remember six months later whether a person or a family or a group actually came through on that day. Even at the large ports, after a cursory medical check, all you need is proof that you have a job or can support yourself and that you aren't a known felon. By air it is even worse. Croydon is so undermanned that passengers can almost step off an aeroplane and stamp their own papers on their way through the customs shed."

211

Croydon. Lucy had an awed thought about actually flying through the air. She looked at Jack. "Have you ever flown?" she asked, distracted by the vision.

His eyes reflected her excitement. "No. Maybe we'll do it together."

Charles swung his legs off the bed and stretched. "I believe this is the point where I take myself downstairs to the bar."

Alone, Jack said, "It was the newspaper report that set Oaks off."

"I thought it might have been," said Lucy. "Gina warned me he wouldn't like it."

"Why did you phone the engagement through if you knew it would cause trouble?"

"Because I was being Phoebe. It was what she would do."

"You're not serious? You, who stepped clear out of cover to warn Gina when Oaks was outside?"

"That was actual. This was theoretical. Did you never do anything against your own character when you were acting a part during the war? Or when you've been undercover? I stepped out when it was immediate, when it was necessary to warn Gina. Not before."

He was silent.

"You do see, don't you?" she said. "I admit the Phoebe money is jolly useful, but also, if I don't act like her when I'm being her, other people might start wondering. It's hard, sustaining two people's characters."

"I'm with you there. I know I said there would be no more deception, but I still have to do it in order to get the journalistic stories."

"I understand."

Jack took a quick breath. "There's more to it than just a job. I survived the war, Lucy. Many of my contemporaries didn't. Many of my father's estate workers didn't. Our villagers didn't. I was cleverer, luckier, more privileged, and I'm still full of guilt for living when so many people I knew died. I have to expiate that. I have to make the world better or what is the point? I love you, Lucy. I want us to be married but I don't know if I have the right to ask you when I am still exorcising my demons, still fighting crime secretly. I don't live a safe life - and I don't feel I've repaid enough of my debt to give up yet."

Relief and exasperation swept through her. "Is that what's been the problem all week? What makes you think you have to do it alone? Why do you have a monopoly on guilt? My cousin was killed on the battlefield while I was at home, helpless. I saw men die in the hospital, Jack. They weren't soldiers, they were boys who'd marched off in an excess of patriotism and realised too late that they were simply battle fodder. The generals didn't care, they didn't know them by name, they were numbers in a trench on a plan, to be pitted against German numbers in a German trench half a field away. I *know* life is never going to be how it was when we were growing up. I know there are new rules, new boundaries and that for some people, wealth is more important than decency. But I don't see why doing our bit, resisting the bad stuff, calling evil out when we find it, should preclude us from being happy."

He took her hands. "Would it make you happy to be married to me?"

She nodded. "It would. Would it make you happy to be married to me?"

"Very much."

"Well then."

He gave a slow smile and drew a box out of his pocket. "Well then, dear Lucy, will you do me the profound honour of becoming my wife?"

She opened the box with fingers that trembled a little. It was an engagement ring. Three graduated peridot gems in a twist of gold. "Jack, it's beautiful."

"It matches your eyes. As soon as I saw it, I knew it had to be the one. It's also genuine Russian workmanship."

She looked up. "Russian?"

"I spotted a waiter I know in Kingsthorpe and followed him to his shop. I don't know what the stones used to be set in and I didn't ask, but there were evidently more of them because he tried to sell me earrings and a pendant to match."

"I wouldn't say no," murmured Lucy, feeling a wash of love for this man who was so much more than he seemed on the surface. She held out her left hand. "Put it on me?"

"Does that mean yes?"

"Of course it means yes." She peeped sideways at him. "I'll have the other pieces as a wedding present."

"That's a relief, because I've already put a down-payment on them. I love you very much, Lucy."

The ring was warm on her finger, as if it had been made for her, as if it was supposed to be there. "I love you too, Jack," she said, and lifted her face to his to seal the promise.

~ ~ The End ~ ~

ACKNOWLEDGEMENTS

My thanks go to the graphic artists of the Golden Age for providing me with a wealth of travel posters to feed my inspiration

My thanks also to Louise Allen for her expertise in spotting plot holes, Sheila Crighton who said she wanted a series, and Kate Johnson for her never-ending support

Thank you to Jane Dixon-Smith for another exactly-right cover

and thank *you*, if I've forgotten to include you

WORKS BY JAN JONES

Full Length Novels

STAGE BY STAGE – Cambridge set romcom featuring a musical theatre company

A QUESTION OF THYME - herbs, healing and humour: love story with WW1 incursions

DIFFERENT RULES - living, loving and growing in a 1990s Bohemian vicarage

MYSTERY ON THE PRINCESS LINE - 1920s ocean liner mystery

MYSTERY AT THE BAY SANDS HOTEL - 1920s coastal resort mystery

~ Newmarket Regencies ~

THE KYDD INHERITANCE – secrets and skulduggery in Regency England

FAIR DECEPTION – secrets and scandal in Regency Newmarket

FORTUNATE WAGER – secrets and sabotage on the Regency racecourse

AN UNCONVENTIONAL ACT – secrets and subterfuge in the Regency theatre

Other novellas

WRITTEN ON THE WIND – trees, old ways &
mobiles set on the N.Yorks moors

FAIRLIGHTS – a pele tower overlooking the sea,
secrets stretching back for years

WHAT THE EYE DOESN'T SEE – a Flora Swift
mystery set in a village post office

AN ORDINARY GIFT – a time-slippish paranormal
romantic mystery, set in Ely

ONLY DANCING – a romantic suspense, with 1970s
flashbacks

(in the pipeline…)

A DISTURBANCE OF SHADOWS - a theatrical
time slip, with very present ghosts

RAVELL'S LUCK - a Regency *Fairlights* story

MYSTERY AT THE BLACK CAT CLUB - 1920s
London mystery

Non Fiction

QL SuperBASIC – the Definitive Handbook

ABOUT THE AUTHOR

Award-winning author Jan Jones was born and brought up in North London, but now lives near Newmarket, equidistant from Cambridge, Bury St Edmunds and Ely. She writes contemporary, mystery, suspense, paranormal and historical romance.

Jan is a vice-president of the Romantic Novelists' Association, who are without doubt the loveliest band of professional writers anywhere on the planet. Their unfailing support and friendship is unrivalled, their parties are legendary and the annual conference is completely unmissable. Website at https://romanticnovelistsassociation.org/

Jan has won the Elizabeth Goudge Trophy twice (in 2002 and 2019), the RNA Joan Hessayon debut novel award in 2005, and has been shortlisted five times in various RoNA Romantic Novel of the Year categories. She writes books, novellas, serials, poetry and short stories for women's magazines. She can be found at http://janjones.blogspot.co.uk/ and is at https://www.facebook.com/jan.jones.7545 for Facebook and on twitter as @janjonesauthor

Fun fact: A former software engineer, Jan co-designed and wrote the Sinclair QL computer language SuperBASIC.

Her textbook *'QL SuperBASIC – the Definitive Handbook'* occasionally turns up in second-hand sales, commanding ridiculous sums of money and causing her to wish quite fervently that she'd kept her original author copies. Thirty years later she retyped, reformatted and re-released a Kindle edition of *'QL SuperBASIC – the Definitive Handbook'*. To her astonishment, and with heartfelt gratitude to all those in the QL community, it is still selling steadily.

Printed in Great Britain
by Amazon